From the Files of

Madison Finn

Read all the books about Madison Finn!

Coming Soon!

From the Files of
Madison Finn

Just Visiting

By Laura Dower

VOLO

HYPERION
New York

For Myles Joseph, our little peanut

Text copyright © 2002 by Laura Dower

From the Files of Madison Finn, Volo, and the Volo colophon are trademarks of Disney Enterprises, Inc.

Printed in the United States of America

First Edition
1 3 5 7 9 10 8 6 4 2

The main body of text of this book is set in 13-point Frutiger Roman.

ISBN 0-7868-1683-X

Visit www.madisonfinn.com

Madison folded a piece of pink construction paper into a fan. Waving it at her face, she tried to concentrate on her new computer file.

It wasn't easy.

Summer So Far

Rude Awakening:
I don't mind it when vacation is too hot to handle. But who made it eighty degrees in my bedroom?

Pant. Pant. Pant. Pant.
Her dog, Phin, sprawled with his paws stretched out on her bedroom floor. Even he needed to cool off.

"Hang in there, Phinnie," Madison said, scratching the top of his head to calm him down. But he scooted under the bed, tail wagging and tongue flapping.

Pant. Pant. Pant. Pant.

"Mom!" Madison yelled, rising from the desk chair in her bedroom and walking over to the staircase. "MO-O-O-OM!"

School wasn't the only thing out for summer.

The Finn cooling system was out, too.

Mom appeared at the bottom of the stairs, wiping her hands on a towel. "How many times do I have to say this," she started to lecture. "I don't want you screaming at me from upstairs. Please come find me if you want to talk."

"Mom, I'm absolutely *dying* in my room," Madison moaned, still fanning her face. "It's like an oven up here. Even Phinnie's hot."

"I told you the AC repairman will be coming over as soon as he can," Mom explained. "Why don't you bring your laptop downstairs? It's much cooler down here in the kitchen."

Madison didn't feel like moving anywhere, especially not to the kitchen. That was no place to write in her files! She needed to be in her own room with her own stuff. She turned back toward her room and opened the window a crack.

The laptop cursor was blinking, so she started to type again.

Although I am suffering from broken-air-conditioner heatstroke right now, I'll live. After all, we got out of school almost a week ago and it is AWESOME to have all this free time again.

Since the last day of school my BFFs and I have been talking a lot. Aimee is going to dance camp soon like she does every summer, but luckily she has a few more weeks at home. Fiona goes to soccer camp right after the Fourth of July.

On our first summer weekend together, Fiona had a sleepover in her backyard & that was wicked nice. Her dad got this hiking tent and we set it up outside. No bugs could get in, which was a good thing. I really, REALLY hate mosquitoes. We sat up half the night, eating marshmallows and talking in the dark, mostly about boys—of course! But I have decided that I won't EVER reveal my crush on Hart Jones, not even to them even though they are my BFFs. I'm just not ready to admit out loud that I like him. What if he finds out?

While we were at Fiona's, another cool thing happened. Aimee dragged the three of us outside the tent to look at stars and the sky was all speckled and beautiful. We stood there in the moonlight while she pointed out all the constellations.

I'm getting VERY jazzed about the upcoming Fourth of July celebration in Far Hills. It's supposed to be the biggest one ever.

I am soooo there. We ALL will be there.
Even Hart. I hope.

Madison sat back in her chair and sighed. She felt sweatier than sweaty. As she sat there fanning herself, the computer's sleep function clicked on automatically. A brand-new screen saver appeared.

Glug. Glug. Glug. Glug.

Earlier in the day, Madison had downloaded a special summer screen saver program that featured bright tropical fish. The screen made noises as fish swam across the screen: underwater bubbles bubbled, water splashed, and the fish went *glug*. It was a little like the home page on her favorite Web site, bigfishbowl.com.

Madison clicked the space bar on the keyboard. A window appeared that said: "WHAT IS YOUR PASSWORD?" She entered her supersecret password, logged online, and went immediately into her personal e-mailbox. One piece of mail was waiting there, sent by someone very important: Madison's keypal Bigwheels. Madison knew that Bigwheels wasn't writing from her home computer. Her whole family was on a summer road trip down the West Coast of the USA.

Madison wondered: If her parents hadn't gotten divorced, then would *she* be traveling in a camper across the country, too, instead of sitting here in a steamy bedroom?

The phone rang twice. Mom picked it up

downstairs. Madison could barely hear her mumbling into the receiver.

"That was your father!" Mom yelled up a moment later. "Surprise! He's late."

Dad was always late to pick up Madison for their weekly dinners. But Madison didn't mind it—as long as he showed up. Tonight they had made plans to go to their favorite barbecue restaurant together, just the two of them. His girlfriend, Stephanie, had a conflict and couldn't make it. Madison was momentarily disappointed that it wouldn't be *three* for dinner, but decided not to get upset.

It was summer, and she was supposed to be cooling off, not heating up.

She clicked OPEN on her keyboard. Madison could read Bigwheels's e-mail from the road while she waited for Dad.

```
From: Bigwheels
To: MadFinn
Subject: I LOVE SUMMER!!!
Date: Thurs 26 June 2:46 PM
Happy vacation! Aren't you glad
school is OVER? What's up with you?

We're in OREGON now! I am not sure
what the name of the town is. I
have to send you an e-postcard. My
mom is trying to help me figure out
how to download it.
```

We left Washington two days ago
and have been stopping along the
coastline. It is pretty. We have a
special camper and everything. My
sister and I have bunk beds and
there's even a TV set inside. Have
you ever gone on a trip like this?
We are driving all the way through
this state and then down to
northern California, to drive right
over the Golden Gate Bridge in San
Francisco.

Did you ever go shopping for that
new bathing suit? Isn't the day at
the lake coming up soon? How is
Hart? And what are you doing for
the Fourth of July? We're going to
find fireworks somewhere. We'd
better!
Yours till the road trips,
Bigwheels, aka Victoria

p.s. I can still get e-mails here
even though I am not home. So K-I-T
(that means WRITE)!

Just as Madison was about to type a response,
Mom came dashing into her room. Dad had called
again. He'd be there in ten short minutes.
Madison disconnected her laptop, crumpled up

her makeshift pink fan, and went downstairs. It was better to wait outside than inside her warm bedroom. The breeze was picking up.

On the Finn porch, Mom had installed a wooden swing seat, and Madison collapsed into its puffy blue cushions. Their house had a western view, so she leaned backward to see if the sun might set while she waited. The whole sky was turning a washed-out yellow, but summer dusk was hours away.

After a few moments, Mom came outside and sat down beside her.

"Did you see Aimee and Fiona today?" Mom asked.

"Nah, but we talked on the phone. Why?" Madison asked back.

"Oh, I don't know. You haven't seen them in a few days and . . . well, I just don't want this to be a summer of you sleeping late and staying inside on the computer all day—"

"Mom," Madison said, interrupting. "What are you talking about? I get out. I walk Phinnie. I've been over to the animal clinic—"

"Once," Mom cut her off. "Now, we just went and bought you that nice new swimsuit. I think you should use it. Aren't you and your friends going to the lake soon? Should we have made camp plans for you?"

Madison made a grouchy face. Every since the "Big D," her parents' divorce, Mom was overly

7

worried about everything Madison did and did not do.

"I'm superfine the way I am," Madison said. "Besides, the Fourth of July is coming up, and we're going to help the parks department with the setup. They ask for junior-high volunteers. That way we all see fireworks up close."

"Well," Mom continued. "We need to talk about the Fourth of July."

Silently Madison dragged her feet along the ground so the swing moved back and forth. She had a sneaking suspicion that she did not want to hear the next part of what Mom had to say.

Mom kept talking. "Unfortunately, I have to work on an important business presentation next week—and then I have to fly out and present it—"

"Like when?" Madison asked.

"Well . . . around the Fourth of July," Mom replied. "It's bad timing, I know. . . ."

"Bad timing? IT'S AWFUL!" Madison blurted, her face swelling up pink. "I can't miss the Fourth of July."

"Maddie . . . honey bear . . ." Mom said, reaching out for Madison's arm, but Madison pulled away.

"Just because you have work, why do I have to leave, too? When were you going to tell me? Can I at least stay with Daddy?" Madison asked three questions all at once.

Mom shook her head. "No, I checked—your father has a business commitment on the other coast that he can't avoid. And I asked Aimee's mom if you could sleep over with them, but they have several guests coming from out of town, too. Oh, Maddie, it's just one of those things. I'm sorry."

Madison's face was all puffy.

"You don't understand, Mom," Madison said. Her knees locked and the swing stopped. "This is the most important Fourth of July ever . . . in my whole entire life. I can't miss it."

"I'm sorry. But we'll make other arrangements. . . ." Mom's voice drifted off.

"What *kind* of arrangements?" Madison asked.

Mom put her hand on Madison's back. "I think you should go to Gramma Helen's for the Fourth of July. And she loves the idea. We can fly out to Chicago together, and then I'll go on to my business trip. . . ."

Madison stood up and threw her arms into the air. "Are you kidding, Mom? Leave my friends to go hang with Gramma Helen? No way."

Mom nodded. "I know it doesn't sound perfect, but it will be just for a week or so. Gramma keeps saying how much she misses you, and how she wants to see you."

"A WEEK?" Madison said. She leaned back in the swing seat and sighed a deep, sad sigh.

No Far Hills carnival? No parade? She'd miss the fireworks?

She'd miss her friends.

Mom and Madison sat there, not speaking for a moment or two. There was total silence except for the sound of Phin's panting.

"Maddie," Mom finally said. "This doesn't have to be a tragedy."

"Easy for you to say." Madison groaned. She felt like crying and screaming at the same time. The Fourth of July was her big chance to hang out with Hart Jones. Now those hopes were dashed.

Phinnie started to howl a little, as if he knew something was wrong. He sniffed at Madison's sneakers.

"Rowrrooooooo!"

"I really am sorry, Maddie," Mom said again. She rubbed the top of Madison's back the way she always did when Madison felt sad or sick.

"You just don't understand, Mom. I can't spend the Fourth of July with my grandmother! The only people around her are old. I'll be so left out. And all my friends are here, not there. I don't know anyone there."

"That's not true," Mom said with a gentle smile.

"MOM! Can't you just postpone your work for a change?" Madison said. She bit her lip.

"No, that is not an option," Mom answered.

"You don't get it!" Madison screamed. Her voice was getting louder and louder.

"Okay, enough yelling, young lady. I think you're

overreacting. Look, it's only a short stay. There are fireworks and carnivals where Gramma lives, too. And you may not believe me, but summers at Gramma's lake house can be pleasantly surprising," Mom said. "I promise."

Madison didn't respond with more than a pout. Dad's car was pulling into the driveway at that exact moment.

She skipped down the porch stairs without really saying a proper good-bye.

Phin howled after her, but Mom held on to his dog collar so he stayed on the porch.

"I love you, Maddie," Mom called out.

"Yeah, I love you, too," Madison replied softly. But she didn't look back. She opened her dad's car door and climbed inside.

Somehow Madison hoped that Dad would have a magical solution that could help her figure out the way to stay home, sweet home, for the Fourth of July.

It would take serious magic to save this summer.

Chapter 2

"What's new?" Dad asked when Madison crawled into his car.

She wanted to blurt out everything she was thinking but was afraid it would all come rushing out like a big mess.

"Cat got your tongue?" Dad asked. "Or should I say, *dog* got your tongue?" He laughed at his own dumb joke.

But Madison still didn't laugh or speak.

"How are you feeling, honey?" Dad asked.

"Mmmnh . . . fine," Madison grunted back at Dad.

"Well," Dad said, clearing his throat. "You don't sound very fine."

"Yeah," Madison said. "Guess not." She gazed out the passenger-side window. They drove past a few more houses before turning into the downtown area of Far Hills where the barbecue restaurant was.

"What is it, Maddie?" Dad asked, seriously now. He reached out for Madison's knee. "You can tell me."

Madison realized she couldn't keep her feelings hidden all night, so she spoke up. Her voice quivering a little, she explained about the Fourth of July fiasco and the pending trip to Gramma Helen's lake house. She hoped that Dad would just fix things— and be on Madison's side.

Unfortunately, Dad wouldn't. He just stared straight ahead, driving slowly toward their BBQ destination.

"Gee, now *I* don't know what to say, Maddie," he blurted after a brief pause. "Your mother . . . well, she works pretty hard. I know she isn't ruining your Fourth of July on purpose. And I'd change my work schedule if I could . . . but I can't, either. I don't know what to tell you. . . ."

Madison crossed her arms and sighed.

What would Bigwheels do in a situation like this? Madison wished her keypal were there right now to help her through this muddle. Didn't parents understand *anything* about the importance of a perfect summer vacation?

"I'm surprised you don't think staying with Gramma Helen could be fun," Dad continued. "She has that great house by Lake Michigan. Nice neighbors. Ducks. There's a lot to do up there. . . ."

"Ducks?" Madison shot him a look. "What am I supposed to do with ducks? Dad, out there is not as much fun as here with Aimee and Fiona."

Dad wasn't sure how to respond to *that*. "I know," he said simply.

He silently pulled into the barbecue restaurant parking lot and parked the car. In front of them, Madison noticed a giant billboard.

"Just look at that," she moaned to Dad as she read the sign aloud.

FAR HILLS INDEPENDENCE DAY EXTRAVAGANZA!
FREE RIDES! FREE RAFFLES! FREE FUN!
DOWNTOWN CENTER, JULY 4
12 PM TO 10 PM
GAMES ALL DAY! FIREWORKS ALL NIGHT!

Her heart sank even lower than before.

"Now, sweetheart, don't get upset. I'll bet there's an 'extravaganza' at Gramma Helen's, too," Dad said, trying to be reassuring. "I'll bet they have rides and games all day there, too."

"But who will I go on the rides with, Dad? Ride a roller coaster with Gramma Helen?" Madison asked. "I don't think so."

Dad shrugged. "Well, you can watch the fireworks from Gramma's," he said. "And I'll bet Mom will let you bring Phinnie along for the trip. You and Phin can light sparklers together. . . ."

Madison sighed. Bringing Phin would help the situation, but a pug was no replacement for a real BFF.

"Let's go get some food, and we can talk more," Dad said, gently grabbing Madison's shoulder.

Madison squirmed.

How could anyone eat BBQ at a time like this?

But she went anyway.

Surprisingly, after a few spicy french fries (and a few more of Dad's dumber-than-dumb jokes), Madison's spirits lifted a little. And by the time he suggested they go for dessert at Freeze Palace, Madison was actually grinning from ear to ear. Ice cream was happy food, after all. A person couldn't be sad and lick a waffle ice-cream cone at the same time. Madison couldn't.

As usual, the line for Freeze Palace was out the door on a warm summer night, but Madison didn't mind waiting. She'd only been standing there for a few moments when Aimee appeared with two of her brothers, Dean and Billy.

"Maddie!" Aimee squealed as soon as she saw her best friend. She greeted Madison's dad, too. "Hey, Mr. Finn!"

Madison gave her BFF a big squeeze. "What are you doing here?"

"Pigging out!" Aimee said, laughing. She was always going on and off diets, but in the summer even ballerina Aimee couldn't resist ice cream. And

Freeze Palace made the best chocolate cow (aka superthick mocha milk shake) in town.

"Did you guys walk here all the way from your house?" Madison asked.

"Yes, and . . ." Aimee pulled Madison a little off to one side. "Do you know who I just saw on the way?"

Aimee broke into giggles.

"Who?" Madison asked, impatient. "Tell me. TELL ME!"

"Ben Buckley!" Aimee squealed. She covered up her mouth to pretend that no one could hear.

Madison smiled. "I thought you stopped crushing on him!" she said.

Aimee blushed. "Me, too. But then he stopped to say hello to me even though he was with his friends. That means something, right? My brothers even said he seemed extra nice, and they *never* say stuff like that."

Boys liked Aimee and Aimee loved boys, especially brainiacs. Ben was the smartest kid in the seventh grade. Up until now, he hadn't really shown an interest in her.

"So are you two going out this summer or something?" Madison teased.

"No way!" Aimee cut her off. "OH MY GOD! We just said hello, Maddie—it was really no biggie," Aimee cried, blushing some more.

The ice-cream line started moving faster now.

Madison's dad, who had been chatting with the Gillespie brothers, put his arm around Madison and moved them all forward a few paces.

"So what's your family doing for Independence Day?" Dad asked Aimee.

Madison elbowed him. "Dad!" she said.

He realized immediately that he'd asked the wrong question.

Aimee replied instantly. "Oh my God! My friend Sasha from dance camp is coming into town," she explained, talking a mile a minute. "And you know she's from Russia . . . well, she lives in New York . . . but oh, we're so excited to hang out together and Maddie, I can't wait for you guys to meet each other! We will have sooo much fun at the carnival and the fireworks and—"

"Aimee," Madison interrupted. "I think I may be going away next week. Change of plans."

"What?" Aimee asked. "You can't go somewhere else!"

Madison sighed. "Yeah, it's a bummer. I'm going to miss the Fourth of July parade and carnival."

Aimee frowned. "I can't believe it!" she cried. "That is totally unfair. Mr. Finn, why can't she stay here?"

Dad made a helpless face as if he didn't know how to answer anything that twelve-year-old girls asked him tonight.

By now the ice-cream line had moved inside the

17

store, but Madison didn't feel much like a frozen treat anymore. She just felt frozen.

"Hey, move it, weasel!" Aimee's brother Dean said, gently shoving Madison up to the counter. He and Billy laughed. Aimee punched them both on behalf of her BFF.

Normally Madison would have laughed too, and shoved back. But tonight, she wanted to run away. Not even Aimee could make her feel better.

Dad got the message loud and clear.

He ordered two supersize chocolate cows—to go.

Later, after dropping off Madison at home, Dad stood on the porch talking to Mom for almost half an hour.

Wasn't there a way to let Madison stay home for the Fourth of July?

Madison eavesdropped on them both through the living-room window, but she didn't hear anything encouraging. Neither parent could afford to change his or her work plans. Everyone else in town was busy with their own houseguests.

So it was decided once and for all.

The Far Hills Fourth of July would have to do without Madison Francesca Finn and Phineas the dog. Phin could go to Gramma's with Madison, which was some consolation. But the extravaganza part of everything was kaput.

Slurping on the last slurp of her chocolate cow,

Madison poked her head out onto the porch to say good night to Mom and Dad. As she climbed the stairs up to her room, Phin followed, nuzzling her legs.

Madison went right over to her laptop. Was anyone on bigfishbowl.com? She'd told Aimee that she'd miss the Fourth of July, and now Madison had to tell the same icky news to Fiona. As she logged online, her buddy list popped up. Both friends were there, so Madison Insta-Messaged them with the name of a private chat room. They had things to discuss.

"Meet me in BFFLAND and hurry," Madison said, waiting impatiently for them to show up.

Fiona got there first.

```
<Wetwinz>: whassup?
<MadFinn>: EOTW
<BalletGrl>: TOTAL 911 maddies parnts
   r unfair!!!
<Wetwinz>: y?
<MadFinn>: I cant go to July 4
<Wetwinz>: WDYS?
<MadFinn>: have to go to my grammas
   instead
<Wetwinz>: u won't be here???
<BalletGrl>: { :-{
<Wetwinz>: me 2!!!
<MadFinn>: ((you guys))
<Wetwinz>: wait but my friend Debbie
   from California is coming I want u
   to meet her
```

Madison sighed. She could feel her BFFs slipping away—even if it was only for a week. Not only would she miss meeting Sasha, but now she'd miss Debbie, too.

```
<MadFinn>: boo hooooooooo
<BalletGrl>: MOM sez u can't stay
   w/us because my whole family will
   be here plus Sasha.
<MadFinn>: Im so bummed
<Wetwinz>: I could ask my mom if u
   can stay w/us
<MadFinn>: no, that's ok my gramma
   thinks I'm coming now so I have
   to go she'll be sad if I don't
<Wetwinz>: :>(
<BalletGrl>: but you'll be at Lake
   Dora right?
```

Madison paused before sending her reply. She had almost forgotten about Lake Dora. A group of friends were meeting there for swimming the next day, Friday afternoon. Everyone who was anyone would be there—including Hart.

```
<MadFinn>: OF COURSE
<Wetwinz>: koolness!!
<BalletGrl>: what r u guys wearing
   there???
<MadFinn>: mom got me a new bathing
   suit
```

```
<Wetwinz>: bikini?
<MadFinn>: LOL
<BalletGrl>: I have a bikni whas
    wrong with Biknis
<MadFinn>: Aim u cant spell!
<Wetwinz>: LOL I have a bikini 2
<MadFinn>: not 4 me—mine is blue
    racer back
<Wetwinz>: I bet it's pretty :>)
<BalletGrl>: what guys r coming?
<Wetwinz>: Chet said egg, drew, dan,
    and hart so far
<BalletGrl>: Oooooh EGG! xoxoxoxox
<Wetwinz>: VVF
```

Madison grinned as she reread the chat lines. Hart would be there. She'd confirmed it. And Fiona was probably grinning, too, since it had been revealed that Walter "Egg" Diaz would also be there. Fiona had been crushing on Egg since she first met him.

Egg had been one of Madison's best guy friends since they were little kids. It was hard to imagine him dating *anyone*.

After a few more minutes chatting about who else would be seen at the lake and what else people would be wearing to the lake, Madison signed off with a "c u tomorrow" and a *poof*. She was feeling sleepy now and needed to finish up her earlier e-mail to Bigwheels before going to bed for the

night. She still owed Bigwheels a reply to her
Oregon e-mail.

From: MadFinn
To: Bigwheels
Subject: Re: I LOVE SUMMER!!!
Date: Thurs 26 June 9:12 PM

Ur trip sounds awesome.

Turns out I will be traveling a
little, too. I just found out today
that I have 2 go to my grandmother's
house for July 4. Sounds good?
Nope. Now I won't be home for
fireworks or Hart or anything. And
you said the Fourth would be my big
chance to see if he liked me or
not!!!

I'm going to the lake tomorrow with
a group of friends, but I don't
think Hart will even notice me
there. It's not romantic like the
Fourth of July, with carnival rides
to go on (you know what I mean,
like in the movies or something).

Oh, I did get the new bathing suit
BTW. It's navy blue, but I think my
legs look jiggly. Do you wear a one
piece or a bikini bathing suit? Why

does everyone always show off their stomach like that? Aimee wants to get a belly-button pierce. You don't have one, do u?

I wish I were in a special camper going all the way across the country like you. Then I wouldn't have to obsess about everything here. What am I going to do at my gramma Helen's house for a whole WEEK? All she does is cook and play crazy eights. If u have ideas, pleez send them now.

I got your e-postcard BTW, but I couldn't open the attachment or the link. Send me another one pronto! I have to find a funny one to send back.

Yours till the swimming pools,
MadFinn, aka Maddie

P.S. Can your camper drive to Chicago? How cool would that be? THEN the Fourth of July would rock. CUL8R.

As Madison hit SEND, a loud *swoosh* roared through her bedroom. But it had nothing to do with her laptop. All at once, a gust of cool air streamed through the air-conditioning vent directly over her desk.

Phinnie even woke up; it was that loud.

Madison smiled when she felt the air—and wondered if this was a good omen for tomorrow. Now that her room was cooling off, could she cool down, too—and have fun at Lake Dora? Or maybe it even meant something *cool* would happen with Hart?

She stood under the vent and let the chilly air blow all over before pulling on her pj's and crawling on top of the covers.

Phin crawled on top, too.

He was asleep in less than a minute.

Chapter 3

Madison stared back at her reflection in the mirror.

She couldn't decide if she wanted to wear the blue or the white T-shirt over her new bathing suit. Finally she decided on blue instead of white (since white was too see-through). She braided her hair and pulled it back with a carved tortoiseshell clip that Mom had bought for her. Last, she slipped on her flowered thongs. Her toenails were painted Seashell Pink, and although they were a little chipped around the edges, they still looked pretty.

"Someone's here for you!" Mom called from the front door. Madison grabbed her straw bag and bolted down the stairs. Aimee was waiting there, arms outstretched.

"You look so cute!" she said when she saw

25

Madison. They left Mom and hopped down the porch steps and into Aimee's brother's car.

"Hey! Don't slam the door!" Dean said as Madison crawled into the backseat. "I just got the paint retouched on that side."

Dean was way into cars, especially this one. He'd rebuilt the engine just last summer. No one was allowed near Dean's car unless he said so.

"And watch the backseat, too," he warned Madison. "I don't want to get sand in the car."

"Just chill out. We haven't even gotten to the beach. Where's the sand coming from?" Aimee yelled at her brother. "Look what I brought," she said, turning around toward the backseat. Aimee produced two giant lemons and smiled, fluffing up her own blond 'do. "For the sun. So I can get blonder hair."

"We have to go pick up Fiona now, right?" Dean groaned. Although Dean was pretty good about giving Aimee and her friends rides in the summertime, he loved to complain.

"Great bikini top," Madison commented on Aimee's suit. "Are those little flowers on it?"

Aimee snapped her top. "Yes! Aren't they pretty? Let me see your new bathing suit, too, Maddie," she said.

Madison lifted her T-shirt to show off the daisy on the center of her suit.

"You have flowers, too!" Aimee squealed, loudly enough to make Dean shoot her a dirty look.

"Could you not scream like that, please?" Dean

asked. He pulled up fast in front of Fiona's house. The brakes screeched.

Fiona barreled out of her front door toward Dean's car and got into the back next to Madison.

"Hi-ya, everyone!" Fiona said. As luck would have it (and since great friends think alike), Fiona's new swimsuit *also* had little flowers on it.

"We all match!" Aimee said, beaming. Madison grinned, too.

"Egg's mom just picked up Chet," Fiona said. "Drew and Hart were in the backseat."

Madison wondered if maybe she should have worn the white T-shirt. Did it look better? Would Hart like it better?

"I am soooo psyched to get on the beach!" Aimee said.

Dean drove onward to Lake Dora. The road to the lake was winding and rocky, and with each bump, Dean touched his dashboard, as if something bad might happen to his precious car.

Aimee got a bad case of the giggles from all the bumpity-bump, but Madison made sure her seat belt was fastened tightly—just in case. Fiona gasped out loud every time the car bounced up and down.

Bumps or no bumps, it was a relief to be out of the house, Madison thought as they drove along. She rolled down the window and inhaled gulps of lakeside air. Some of the trees along this winding road had sprouted white buds among their deep green leaves, and violets bloomed up and down the pavement. She wished she could jump out and pick her own bouquet.

"Does anyone know if Ben Buckley is going to be there?" Aimee asked sheepishly from the front seat. She had her mind on one boy.

Fiona cocked her head to one side and cracked, "Who wants to know?"

Aimee blushed. "Um . . . me?"

No one really knew who would be showing up at the lake, but both Madison and Fiona hoped Ben would make it. Aimee hadn't had a crush like this in a long time. It was all she could think—and talk—about.

"Here we are!" Dean announced, pulling into a parking lot area.

Up ahead, groups of different kids were gathered by the Lake Dora boathouse. Some were choosing life vests and grabbing canoes. Others were standing around staring at one another. Madison recognized a friend from school, Lindsay Frost, standing next to a giant kayak. Egg and Drew were standing close by alongside Egg's mom, Señora Diaz, Spanish teacher at Far Hills Junior High.

Dean pulled his car into an empty spot and then ordered Aimee, Madison, and Fiona "O-U-T!" But he also promised he'd come back to pick everyone up at three o'clock. After a short chorus of good-byes, Dean whirred away, stepping on the gas and disappearing back the way they'd driven in.

"This is so weird," Fiona said. "When I lived in California, hanging out at the beach wasn't like this. We didn't stand around. We played games and talked and . . ."

"That's what we do, too!" Aimee squealed, slipping her arm through Fiona's arm.

Madison pointed across the beach. "There's Dan Ginsburg," she said. He was a friend from school and from the animal clinic where Madison volunteered.

"Hey, I don't see evil Poison Ivy anywhere," Aimee said as she surveyed the beach, too. "That's a good thing, right?"

Ivy was a seventh-grade rival who had a nasty habit of showing up unannounced at group events. Poison Ivy was always accompanied by her duo of drones, Rose Thorn and Phony Joanie. Madison and her crew had dreamed up some awful nicknames for their enemies over the years.

Gradually more and more and MORE cars appeared. Not everyone was dropping off junior high school kids, of course. There were families with toddlers, grandparents with beach chairs and umbrellas, and other people milling about. Madison counted more than twenty different sets of friends and families.

"Hey, you guys," Egg called out, and walked over toward the girls.

His mother waved, too, but then headed in the opposite direction back toward the family car. Like

Dean, she was just dropping off. Most parents and older siblings were doing that, leaving the younger kids to play and swim together. There was freedom at the lake when moms and dads weren't there. Lifeguards kept order, but they didn't hover like *parents*.

Madison welcomed the cool lake air after the week of heat in Far Hills—especially after dealing with the broken air-conditioning unit at home. She poked at her bathing-suited tummy, wondering whether she should get wet or not. Meanwhile boys barreled into the water, screaming, even though no one was supposed to scream. Girls pulled off shorts and T-shirts to reveal a rainbow of different-colored bathing suits.

Lake Dora was set up with a series of three long, interconnected docks for swimming and diving. There was an area reserved for weaker swimmers and toddlers, an area for swimmers who liked doing laps, and a general swim area with a diving platform.

Most of the seventh graders were headed for the free swim area.

Madison stood off to the side, still unsure about whether she felt like getting into the water. She watched as Aimee and Fiona made their way to the docks, yelling for her to follow.

"Nah," Madison yelled back. "I'm just going to hang out here for a little while first."

Lindsay Frost came over, still wearing her T-shirt, too. Madison smiled.

"I hate getting sunburned," Lindsay said, plopping onto a towel and pulling her T-shirt way down over her knees.

Madison sat down beside her. "Me, too," she said, glad that someone else in the group was as self-conscious as she was.

They watched as the kids in the water dove off docks and splashed around, laughing. It did look like fun. Lindsay wasn't budging, but Madison eventually stood up and wandered over to the water's edge.

"COME IN!" Aimee screamed from a dock before leaping into the air and crashing into the water.

Madison saw Chet run up behind his twin sister, Fiona, like he was about to push her in the water, but a lifeguard blew a whistle.

"No running!" the guard called out. "And no pushing, or I'll have to ask you to leave the beach."

Dripping wet, Aimee rushed up to Madison on the shore and grabbed her arm. "You have to come in," she pleaded. "Or at least come sit on the dock. It's so much fun!"

Madison shrugged and waded into the water, still wearing her blue T-shirt. She climbed onto one long dock and followed Aimee over toward the group that was leaping and diving. She kept looking behind her to make sure that Egg and Chet wouldn't push her into the water unexpectedly.

"Hooray!" Fiona squealed. "You're here! Watch this!" She did a perfect swan dive into Lake Dora.

Egg, standing on another dock, clapped for Fiona's dive. No one else seemed to notice except Madison. She was beginning to think that Egg really did like Fiona back.

Boom. Boom. Boom. Boom. SPLASH!

Someone else came running down the dock out of nowhere and jumped into the water right by where Madison was sitting.

Her T-shirt was soaked instantly.

"Good one!" Drew yelled from where he was bobbing in the water.

Hart Jones popped his head up out of the lake.

"Hey, Finnster!" Hart said, treading water.

Madison felt her stomach flip-flop and her cheeks turn a little pink, but luckily she could blame that on the sun.

"Hello, Hart," she replied sheepishly. She couldn't be mad at him right at first for getting her all wet.

Hart kicked his feet and water sprayed around in every direction, especially at Madison. She tried to laugh like he was doing something funny, but she really wasn't very happy about it.

"Could you splash over there?" Madison asked.

Hart just laughed. "Okay, sure." Then he turned around and kicked his feet out again toward Madison. A spray of water came flying her way and she squealed.

"HART!" Madison said.

She stood up, exasperated, and reclipped her

32

soaked hair onto the top of her head, her blue T-shirt now heavy with water. It sucked against her body with the worst pucker and cling ever.

"Sorry!" Hart said, laughing.

Chet gave him a high five.

"It was just a joke, Maddie!" Chet yelled.

Aimee, who'd been watching the splashing, swam over and got revenge on behalf of her BFF. She soaked Hart from where she was treading water.

Splash!

Aimee climbed up onto the dock. "Are you okay?" she asked Madison.

"Yeah, are you okay?" Fiona yelled, swimming over to the other side of the same dock. She treaded water.

Madison nodded. "I'm okay. Just wet."

"Take off your shirt and dive in," Fiona said. "We can get my brother back. I know how."

Madison shook her head and leaned backward, dangling her feet into the lake and wringing the water from her shirt. Out of the corner of her eye, she noticed that Hart was swimming over. Chet was right behind him. Playfully they pretended to splash each other—and then they splashed Madison again instead.

"You guys!" Madison said. "I said, quit it!"

"Quit what, Finnster?" Hart laughed.

"Quit THIS!"

And with one great kick, Madison sent a wave of

water cascading over Hart's head. All the other kids on the docks roared with laughter.

"HA! HA! She got you good," Chet said, chuckling.

The lifeguard blew a whistle. "STOP THAT NOW!" he commanded, coming over to the area where they were swimming. He planted himself on the dock there so everyone would stop acting up once and for all.

Madison smirked and smoothed out her wet hair. The splash fight was *over*, and she was gladder than glad. Unfortunately, something was missing. Madison's hair was loose. With all the splashing, her tortoiseshell clip had flown off into Lake Dora.

Frantically she bent over to see if the clip was floating anywhere nearby, but didn't see it. Hart swam over to see what was wrong, but she barked at him.

"Get away!" Madison cried. "I lost something!" She looked everywhere for the hair clip. It was gone.

Hart tried to help her look, but he gave up after a little while. Madison gave up, too. By now, her blue T-shirt was weighted down and stretched out by the water it had absorbed. It was hanging way down below her bottom. She walked quickly back over to Lindsay on the beach and dug around in her bag for a loose rubber band to pull her hair back up.

"What happened?" Lindsay asked, rubbing some sunblock on her shins. "I saw you guys were splashing each other. . . ."

"Boys are just idiots," Madison said, squeezing some more water out of her shirt. "*And* I lost my favorite hair clip."

Aimee and Fiona came rushing over from the lake and collapsed onto their own towels.

"You missed it, Maddie!" Aimee said. "When that lifeguard turned his back, Fiona finally splashed Hart and Chet back—and good! They got water up their noses and everything."

Fiona laughed. "That was so much fun! My brother and I always get each other like that. You have to be very strategic."

"Yeah, my brothers and I splash a lot, too," Aimee said.

Madison wondered if she hated splashing so much because she didn't have a brother.

"Hart Jones is an awesome swimmer," Aimee said. "Did you see that flip he did in the water?"

Fiona nodded. "Yeah, too bad FHJH doesn't have a swim team. He'll definitely be on the team in high school."

Madison listened as her friends talked about Hart like he was something special. She couldn't understand why, for the first time, she *didn't* feel the same way. Because of him, she'd lost her favorite clip.

"Who wants a snow cone?" Aimee said all of a sudden.

Madison felt hot and damp and didn't really want a snack, but she went for the walk. Fiona and

Lindsay decided to stay behind and talk about soccer camp.

"Don't let me forget, I have to put lemon juice in my hair," Aimee said as they walked to the snow cone stand.

"Uh-huh," Madison said, half listening. She closed her eyes and let the sun warm her face. The blue T-shirt was drying quickly now. She didn't feel quite as self-conscious as before—even without her favorite clip.

"Mmmmmm," Aimee said when she got her treat. "It's grape. Want a bite?"

Madison shook her head and giggled because Aimee's lips and tongue were turning purple with every lick. But Aimee didn't seem to care.

Fiona and Lindsay had disappeared by the time they came back to the towels, so Aimee and Madison just sat down to relax for a while. Madison saw Hart sitting a few yards away, and she was pretty sure he was waving, trying to get her attention.

But she ignored him and waved to Drew instead, who was passing by at that exact moment. He came over and sat near the girls.

"This is cool, being here at the beach with everyone, right?" he said. Drew was the one who'd organized the Lake Dora outing in the first place. He was always planning events like pool parties and minigolf games at his parents' house and other places in Far Hills.

Aimee licked her snow cone and nodded.

Madison raised an eyebrow. "I guess so," she said. "Like when I'm not getting splash attacked."

Drew chuckled. "Oh yeah, I saw that."

"Yeah," Madison said. "Very funny."

"Either of you guys going to camp this year?" Drew asked.

Aimee spoke up immediately about ballet camp starting in only a few weeks. Drew then told them how he was headed to archery camp this summer. It was a toss-up between that and computer camp, and he'd picked archery.

Madison didn't have any camp plans, so she didn't have much to contribute to the conversation. As Drew kept talking, her thoughts drifted off and she started to make a minicastle out of the sand on her right side. A piece of paper blew over where she was digging.

Drew snatched it.

"'July Fourth Extravaganza!'" he read aloud from the flyer. "Oh, man, this is going to be the biggest blast *ever*, don't you think?" He turned the paper around to show it off to Madison and Aimee. "Aren't you psyched, Maddie?"

Madison frowned.

After all, she wasn't going to the blast. She was going to Gramma's.

Not even a beautiful sunny day at the lake could change that.

Chapter 4

"Give that to me," Aimee said, taking the flyer out of Drew's hand.

"Don't grab!" he said. "What's your problem?"

"Drew, we can't talk about this right now," Aimee whispered. "Maddie can't go to the Fourth of July this year."

Drew turned to face Madison. "Oh, wow," he said. "How come?"

"I just have to go to my gramma's house in Winnetka," she explained.

"Where's Winnetka?" Drew asked.

"Near Chicago," Madison said. "Far away."

"That really stinks," he said.

Aimee socked him on the shoulder. "Shut up, Drew," she said. "Are you trying to make her feel worse?"

Madison sighed. She didn't need help feeling worse.

"Sorry 'bout that," Drew said.

The sun—and the subject matter—were getting superhot by now. Drew suggested that maybe they could go for a ride on the paddleboat to cool off.

Madison wanted to stay away from the water. She said no.

Aimee jumped right up. "I'll go," she said, standing up and brushing the sand off her bottom. "Sure you don't want to go, Maddie?"

Madison shook her head no again and leaned back on her elbows to watch the lifeguards instead. Leaning backward was the best way to lie on a beach towel. It made her stomach look flatter.

But she wasn't left alone for long. Moments after Aimee and Drew walked off to the boathouse, Fiona and Lindsay came back.

"Hey!" Fiona said, sitting down on her towel. "What are you staring at?"

"That lifeguard," Madison said, cupping her hand over her eyes so she could see him better through the sun glare. "He's kind of cute."

Fiona smirked. "Earlier today, that one said I was a good swimmer," she said proudly. "And he's not *kind of* cute. He is wicked cute."

Lindsay laughed. "He's cuter than Egg," she said.

Fiona fake-punched her and laughed. "Gosh,

does everyone on the planet know that I like Walter?" she said, using his real name.

"Walter?" Madison said, sitting up. "Fiona, no one calls him that but his mother."

"Well, I think Egg is a dumb nickname," Fiona said. "It makes him sound like an egghead or something."

Of course, that was the whole idea. Aimee and Madison had nicknamed him that way back in elementary school after he got egged in the head by kids playing a Halloween prank.

"I think you guys should go on a real date," Lindsay said. "He obviously likes you, too."

Fiona gulped. Madison couldn't believe Lindsay would say that right out in public, but she did.

"No way, Lindsay!" Fiona said, embarrassed. "Besides, I'm leaving for soccer camp, and he's off to computer camp soon. And my mom and dad won't let me go on a real date. Do yours?"

"Who's going to ask me on a real date?" Lindsay asked.

Madison started to say, "Who wouldn't?" but she cut herself short. Egg was walking toward them at that exact moment—and Hart was following right behind him.

"Hey," Egg said, smiling in Fiona's direction. "Some of us were thinking about playing volleyball. You want to join in? I mean, all three of you."

Madison smiled. "Sure," she said for the three of them.

"Cool," Hart said, looking right at Madison.

"Yeah, cool," Egg said, turning to Hart. "That means we've got me, you, Drew when he comes back in, Dan, Lance, Chet, Fiona, Lindsay, Aimee, Maddie, Ivy, and Joanie."

"Ivy?" Madison said aloud without realizing it.

"Yeah." Egg pointed over to the refreshment area. "She and Joanie just got here a little while ago."

Fiona rolled her eyes. "Whatever," she said.

"What's the big deal?" Egg asked.

Fiona shook her head and huffed. Madison and Lindsay let out a little sigh. After so many years of being friends, Madison couldn't believe Egg remained so dense about their biggest seventh-grade rival. When was he going to learn once and for all that Ivy was the ENEMY?

Hart was no better. He just smiled. "That's cool," he said, having no clue about what was the matter.

The boys told all three girls to meet them over by the volleyball net on the other side of the beach in a few minutes.

"Oh my GOD! Who invited *her*?" Aimee asked when she saw Ivy primping and prancing around in her neon bikini top and short shorts.

"Don't ask," Fiona said. "Egg did. Maybe I don't like him as much as I thought I did."

"Could her shorts be any shorter?" Lindsay asked.

Madison let out a big "HA!" and took her place

on the side of the net where she'd been assigned. As fate would have it, Ivy took her own position right next to Madison.

"I'm so bad at volleyball," Ivy said, tugging at her top. Madison had a sudden vision of Ivy crashing into the net, into the sand, and losing her top in front of the entire world—only to slink away in shame. . . .

But that was just a dream. Ivy's top wasn't going anywhere. And neither was Ivy.

The first serves and setups were mellow. Madison's side—calling themselves the Kings—went ahead by three points. Hart was serving, and even Madison had to admit that he was really good.

"Way to go, Hart," she shouted, clapping. It seemed like the supportive thing to do. However, instead of helping, it distracted him. Hart sent his next service directly into the sand with a *pow!*

"Way to go, Maddie," Ivy teased, clapping.

Madison didn't say a word as they rotated positions.

On the other side of the net—calling themselves the Supertanks—Aimee and Fiona jumped around excitedly. Fiona was ready to serve, and she sent the ball soaring over the net with an overhand smash.

Ivy stepped to the side when it came over, leaving Madison alone to get it back. Madison dove—and missed. She landed face down in the sand.

"Oh, jeez!" Dan said from behind. "What happened there?"

Madison picked herself up from the sand and gave Ivy an evil stare.

And then the same exact thing happened again with the next serve.

"Get the ball once in a while, Ivy," Madison said. "Instead of running away from it?"

Ivy threw her hands into the air. "It was on your side. I didn't want to interfere," she said.

Hart spoke up from behind them. "That really was your ball, Maddie."

Madison wanted to run away as soon as he said that. But she gritted her teeth and stayed put. Luckily, by the time her own turn to serve came up, she got two points right away. Even Ivy couldn't argue with success. On the next go-around, all of Ivy's serves went *under* the net.

After a few more rounds, someone yelled out that it was almost two-thirty. Madison and the rest of the group started to head back toward the docks for one last swim or canoe ride.

"So—are you guys going swimming?" Ivy asked. "Me and Joanie are. Since we got here late, I mean."

Hart turned to Madison. "Want to go back in the water?" he asked her.

"Uh, no," Madison said quietly.

"I promise I won't splash you this time," Hart said.

Ivy chuckled.

Madison wanted to slug them both.

"Well," Hart said. "I'll see you later."

"Yeah, later, Maddie," Ivy said. She had gotten what she wanted. Ivy ran ahead to the lake without any competition.

While Madison kept her distance from the docks, Aimee and Fiona raced to take a kayak out for one last go around the lake. Madison sat down on her towel and just stared out at the water, wishing that she didn't have to leave these friends and head to Chicago that weekend. The lake had turned so many shades of blue during the day. Just like Madison felt.

Out of nowhere, Hart appeared.

"Good volleyball game, Finnster," Hart said, sitting down right next to Madison on the sand.

She looked up, surprised. "Thanks, I guess," she said.

They sat in silence for a moment or two.

"Hey, I like your T-shirt," Hart said, tugging at its edge.

Madison pulled away a teeny bit. "Yeah, it got all wet before, but the sun dried it out. I guess it's silly that I didn't just take it—"

"Huh?" Hart asked, distracted.

"Nothing," Madison said. *Was he listening to her?*

"Aimee told me you won't be at the Fourth of July," Hart said.

"No," Madison sighed dejectedly.

"Bummer," Hart said. "Everyone's going to be there. It would be cool—"

Splash! Splash!

"Aaah!" Madison wailed.

While Hart had been talking, Madison had gotten doused with a bucketful of water. Her hair dripped wet.

Egg jumped out from behind, cracking up. He was holding an empty pail of water. Chet was standing next to him laughing just as hard. Hart couldn't help but laugh, too.

"Why did you do that?" Madison screamed. She felt a surge of summer heat inside herself—nerves, anger, and most of all, embarrassment.

"Lighten up, Maddie," Egg said. "It's just for fun!"

Madison threw a fistful of sand toward him, missing completely.

Had Hart just been the decoy? Madison looked at Hart as he ran off behind Egg and Chet. She stood up and wrung out the bottom of her T-shirt.

"Hey, Madison!"

Madison looked up. Hart was running back over to her.

"I almost forgot," Hart said, tossing something onto the towel next to Madison. "I found this before. I think it's yours."

He ran off to the dock, quickly diving into the water before Madison even had a chance to say a word back.

She sighed when she saw what he'd left behind. There on the towel was the tortoiseshell hair clip she'd lost hours before.

Back home that night, a slightly sunburned Madison searched her e-mailbox for a new e-card from Bigwheels. But there wasn't any. In fact, Madison didn't have any mail at all, which was rather depressing, considering that it was summer. Didn't everyone write on his or her computer as much as she did?

The home page on her favorite Web site, bigfishbowl.com, announced special summer chat rooms, a what-I-did-for-my-summer-vacation writing contest (Madison was thinking about entering that one), and, of course, "Ask the Blowfish." This was the advice section of the site. She clicked on a puffy-looking fish swimming around on-screen. When a bubble appeared, she punched in a superimportant question about life. After that, all she had to do was wait for a wise, fishy fortune to appear.

She typed: *Will I have a good time at Gramma's for the Fourth of July?*

The fish swam upside down with its answer. *You've gone overboard.*

Madison frowned. Disappointed, she asked the same question again.

The second time, the fish said, T*hings will go swimmingly.*

Madison looked down at Phin, who'd curled up

by her fuzzy monkey slippers. He was snoring. "What is this fish talking about, Phinnie?" she asked the dog, as if he'd give her a better answer than a cartoon blowfish. Madison couldn't imagine how anything at Gramma's could go "swimmingly."

She typed in a *new* question the next time.

Does Hart like Ivy?

The fish said, *Be careful where you tread water.*

Madison gasped aloud. Was the fish talking about Ivy? Was Madison supposed to be careful of her enemy?

She had to ask that question a second time to know for sure. She was a little more specific then.

Does Hart like Madison?

Now the fish said, *Watch out for sharks.*

Madison gasped louder than before. This blowfish *had* to be talking about Poison Ivy; she knew it! Her head spun with frantic thoughts of Hart and Ivy and the Fourth of July extravaganza. She imagined the worst.

There were so many reasons to be sad about leaving town for the holiday.

Was this one more to add to the list?

Phinnie stirred by Madison's feet with a soft little cry. His wet nose was tickling her ankle. She was so tired from her long day in the sun and the yucky "Ask the Blowfish" advice, and she really wanted to get off the site.

But she typed in one more question, just

for fun . . . just to see what the blowfish would say.

So what is my destiny this summer?

The blowfish replied instantly with an underwater pop: *You will be drowning in a sea of love.*

"HA!" Madison laughed out loud at the computer screen. "Double HA!" After a day at Lake Dora, she was fairly certain that "sea" did not include Hart "Splasher" Jones.

"Rowrrooooooo!" Phin jumped up, collar jangling.

She couldn't trust *anything* the silly blowfish had to say. But after its last answer, she also couldn't wipe the smile off her face.

Chapter 5

Madison watched the Weather Channel with Mom for two days after the Lake Dora get-together, hoping to figure out what to bring to Chicago. She had no idea how to pack for Gramma Helen's lake house. It was getting down to the wire, too. She and Mom were scheduled to leave *that* morning.

Mom pestered Madison to throw some clothes—any clothes—into a bag, but nothing seemed color-coordinated or comfortable enough.

Packing for herself was only half the problem. Madison also had to consider what chew toys and pillows to bring for Phinnie. He'd be riding with baggage on the flight to Gramma's, but Madison still packed him a little suitcase of his very own. His favorite tuggy rope, frayed and smelly, had to be sealed in a plastic bag.

With Mom's help, Madison finally decided on a few colored tank tops, T-shirts, and shorts. She threw in a flowered dress, faded jeans, and a lacy blue summer shirt that Fiona had let her borrow—just in case she and Gramma went somewhere special. Of course, she added in all the other essentials, too: underwear, hair dryer, hair stuff, pj's, sandals, sneakers, and her favorite moonstone earrings.

The suitcase was bursting by the time Mom announced, "We're leaving in twenty minutes!"

Phinnie was panting and running all over the house, too, like he knew something special was about to happen.

Aimee and Fiona stopped by to say good-bye in the nick of time. Mom kept an eye on her watch as the BFFs stood on the porch, exchanging hugs and tearful farewells.

"Promise me you'll e-mail!" Madison asked them both. They nodded.

"You better write, too!" Fiona said.

Madison knew that Aimee and Fiona would be busier than busy with their visitors from out of town, Sasha and Debbie. But she hoped they would write.

"It won't be the same Fourth of July without you!" Fiona wailed. She was starting to tear up.

"Girls, I'm afraid Maddie and I have to go," Mom said, quietly interrupting. "We have a few errands to do before we head to the airport."

Madison wiped a tear from her cheek and

sniffled. "I love you guys," she said. "I'm going to miss you soooooo much." It was only a week, but Madison and her BFFs were closer than close.

They clinched for another group hug before Aimee and Fiona skipped down the porch stairs and onto the sidewalk. Phin barked after them. Madison kept waving until they were well out of sight.

After loading their suitcases into the car, Madison put on Phin's leash and got into the backseat with him. Their first errand was to stop over at the animal clinic where Madison volunteered. Her friend Dan's mom, Eileen Ginsburg, was a nurse at the clinic and had agreed to loan Madison the required doggy travel crate for the plane ride to Chicago.

When they picked up the crate, Eileen had packed it with water, kibble, cookies, and a brand-new rawhide bone. Phin licked his chops and crawled inside without a struggle. He *liked* the crate. The baggage handlers had no problems loading a crated Phin when the time came. He was panting like crazy, and looked almost like he was smiling.

After dropping off the dog, Madison followed Mom toward the sign that said GATES 4A THROUGH 24A. They were in the A terminal, gate 22, all the way at the end of a long walkway. Madison was happy her carry-on backpack had little wheels so she could drag it behind her. They lined up at three different security checkpoints along the way to give their names and show a photo ID.

When Madison and Mom finally took their seats on the plane, it started making a series of insectlike swooshing and whirring noises. Madison looked through the teeny window to her right to see the bunch of panels and flaps lifted and lowered while the plane readied itself for takeoff. She'd been on planes many times before today, but something about leaving home this time had her more appre- hensive than before.

"These seats sure are snug," Mom complained, shifting from side to side. Mom was on the aisle. Madison was on the window. No one would have to sit between them. Center seats on a plane were way too cramped for comfort.

"Please put your tray tables and seats in the upright, locked position," the flight attendant announced over the intercom. He explained the safety rules while other flight attendants went around to check on the passengers.

Madison watched out the window as the plane began its slow roll away from the airport. She'd spent the better part of the last few days thinking and rethinking about the Fourth of July extravaganza —and how she wouldn't be attending. But right then, at that moment when the plane taxied down the runway for liftoff, Madison felt the enormous sadness well up in her all over again.

"You okay, honey bear?" Mom said, leaning over and squeezing Madison's hand.

Madison nodded and tried to hide the fact that she was about to start crying.

"After the plane takes off, you can have a soda and some pretzels," Mom said, as if snack food could wipe away the tears.

Madison squeezed Mom's hand back.

The pilot got on the loudspeaker and explained the flight route they'd be taking. No sooner had he signed off than everyone in the cabin felt the plane rush forward. Takeoff had come at last. Madison was on her way to Chicago for real. There was absolutely no running away now. They were about to soar twenty-five thousand feet into the air.

Bling. Bling. The "fasten seat belt" sign blinked.

Madison closed her eyes as the plane ascended. Mom did, too. After they'd climbed into the air for a little while, Mom turned to her daughter with a comforting voice.

"You know, Maddie," Mom began. "This brings back incredible memories for me. . . ."

Madison sighed. "It does?"

"Going to the lake house was the highlight of every summer when I was your age. We had so much fun there," Mom said.

"You did?"

"Oh yeah." Mom nodded. She was talking about herself and her sister. They were close in age.

"What did you do there?" Madison asked.

"Everything," Mom replied. "Swam, sailed, fished, played checkers . . ."

"Checkers?" Madison asked. "Sounds like a party . . ."

"Hey." Mom giggled. "You know what I mean. And we did other stuff, too. I met the first boy I ever liked—really liked—up at that lake house. His name was Ethan Randall. He was so cute."

Madison couldn't help thinking about Hart Jones right then.

"Well . . . Ethan Randall was the cutest boy I had ever met. And he was so nice, too." Mom smiled. "We went for walks. We swam together in the lake up there. When I was thirteen, I had my best summer ever."

"You did?" Madison said. Madison figured that "best" meant more than just a great game of checkers. "So what happened?"

Mom got a look on her face that flushed her cheeks pink. She knew that look. It was a blush, like the way she'd felt at the beach with Hart.

"Mom . . ." Madison teased. "Tell me what happened!"

Mom looked Madison right in the eye. "It was magic. Sometimes boys can do that to you."

"I know," Madison said. "I thought I was going to have something magical happen at home for the Fourth of July. That's why I'm so sad to go so far away. . . ." she explained.

"So *that's* why you were so angry," Mom said, understanding Madison's moodiness at last. "Your father and I were worried about you. We didn't know why you were so upset about leaving."

"Well, I'm going to miss my friends," Madison said.

"And Hart?'" Mom asked with a little smile.

Madison chewed on her lip and nodded. "He's this boy in my class."

"Hmmm," Mom said. "Well, you know, honey bear, he'll be in Far Hills when you get back. You're only going to be gone for a week. I wouldn't worry about it too much. Summers are filled with all kinds of surprises."

Bling. Bling.

Mom unhooked her seat belt and got up to use the lavatory as soon as the plane beeped.

"It is safe to move around the cabin now," the flight attendant said over the loudspeaker.

Madison turned to look out the window again. Gazing off at the thick clouds, she fell fast asleep.

"Wake up," Mom whispered. "We're landing."

Madison couldn't believe she'd slept through the entire flight. She had planned to write in her files on her laptop and maybe even read a chapter or two from *Just as Long as We're Together*, her favorite book by Judy Blume. But none of that happened. She'd even slept through the refreshment cart.

"Gramma is meeting us at the gate," Mom explained. "You and she will go off to the lake house together while I get on my connecting flight for California. Oh, honey bear, I'm going to miss you!"

"I'll miss you, too, Mom!" Madison said. "But I guess it's just a week."

Mom grinned. "Right you are."

It was a bumpy landing, but Mom and Madison laughed their way through it. Madison wondered if Phinnie had fared as well. She had thoughts of him bumping around inside his carrier, howling at the suitcases in the luggage compartment.

When they pulled into the gate, Madison raced up the gangway and into the terminal. Now that she was here in Chicago, she couldn't wait to see her Gramma Helen. She wanted to throw her arms around Gramma and *hug*.

Mom followed right behind Madison. Her connecting plane was due to board in less than an hour.

"Frannie! Maddie!" Gramma called out when she saw her daughter and granddaughter. She was wearing a floppy purple hat and waving her hands madly in the air. "Over he-ere!"

Madison raced into Gramma Helen's arms.

"Gramma!" she cried. "I'm so happy to see you."

Mom came over and gave her a kiss, too. "Hey, Ma," Mom said, adjusting the strap on her bag. "I hate to say hello and run—but my flight takes off in a little while, so. . . ."

"No time for a cup of coffee or a little chat?" Gramma Helen said. She sounded disappointed.

"I'm sorry," Mom said, taking Gramma's hand. "Can we talk later? I owe you one." They hugged and then Mom turned to Madison.

Madison slid her arms around Mom's waist. "I'll miss you."

Mom kissed Madison's head. "Me, too. Now, be good, Maddie, okay?" She started walking away. "I'll call you when I get into San Francisco—both of you. Love you!"

"Bye!" Gramma and Madison said at the same time. They watched as Mom vanished into a crowd of rushing passengers. Madison kept looking in the same direction, just in case Mom turned around again. Their good-byes had been so fast.

Gramma Helen clapped. "Let me look at you!" She turned Madison around so she saw her front, sides, and back. "You're so BIG!" Gramma said.

Madison felt like she was being inspected. "Big?" she asked, squirming a little.

"I mean . . . *gorgeous!*" Gramma Helen corrected herself. "Mature. Sophisticated! Amazing!"

Madison giggled. "Yeah, sure, Gramma."

"Now, let's get the pooch and get ourselves to Winnetka," she said. It was only a short drive to the community where Gramma lived on the North Shore of Chicago.

"I can't wait for you to see Phinnie!" Madison exclaimed. "He's gotten big, too!"

Gramma Helen grabbed Madison by the shoulders. "We'll get your bag and Phin, and then I thought we could head back to the house and catch up a bit. But we have to stop at the grocery store first. Oh! There's so much to do!"

The baggage claim area was packed with passengers from flights all over the country. People were shoving and elbowing to get a front-row look at the luggage carousels. Gramma stood back and to the side.

"Does Phin come out on this?" Madison asked.

Gramma shook her head. "Nope," she explained. "Comes through this door back here."

She pointed to a metal door with a coded alarm on the lock. Madison stared at the knob until a handler finally came through with a dog carrier. Inside was a Pekinese, and he was acting yippy.

Madison looked up at Gramma. "But where's Phinnie?" she asked. As soon as she said the words, the handler came in again, lugging Phinnie's crate.

"Rowrooooo!" Phin barked as soon as he was brought into the terminal. "Woooooooorf!"

Madison ran over to the crate and peered through the bars. "PHINNIE!"

"Rowrooooo!" Phin barked again.

The handler helped Madison unhitch the crate and reattach Phin's leash. The pug was twirling and twisting all over the place. Once out of the crate, the first thing he did was scoot right over to Gramma Helen, and give her a big lick on the face.

"Oooooooh!" Gramma squealed. "Stinky little dog kissies! How delightful."

Madison chuckled.

In Gramma's world, *everything* was delightful.

Chapter 6

Gramma Helen's car smelled like roses. *Lots* of roses. Madison noticed a funky air freshener die-cut in the shape of a red flower. It was hanging from the dashboard. The smell was overpowering. Even Phin was sneezing.

Their first stop after leaving the airport was the supermarket. Gramma needed milk and some other basic food groups. They parked in the shade, cracked open a window, and left Phin in the car.

Everything about the store was different from Far Hills. Little tables were set up all over the place where people could taste samples of top-selling food items and read magazines. It was like a supermarket library and café in one.

Shopping with Gramma was an adventure. Anytime Madison pointed out that she liked something, it got tossed into the cart. Madison didn't mind being spoiled, though.

Madison marveled at how everyone in the store seemed like Gramma's oldest friend. She'd never considered that her grandmother would have BFFs the same as she did.

On the way out of the market, Madison spotted a red-white-and-blue poster tacked to a bulletin board. It looked a little like the billboard outside the BBQ restaurant and the flyer from the beach back in Far Hills—only this one said much more. Just as Dad had predicted.

Winnetka was holding its own Fourth of July extravaganza with a carnival, BBQ, and fireworks, too. Madison wondered if maybe the celebration here could possibly be *better* than the one back home.

As she and Gramma drove from the store toward the house on the lake, Madison rolled down the window and took some deep breaths. Even the air was different here. Gramma described the places in town as they passed: city hall, the *real* library, her favorite florist shop, and even a pet shop.

"Hey, look, Phin!" Madison cried out. "A pet store!"

Phinnie barked from the backseat.

"It's so peaceful here," Madison said to Gramma. After driving for only a few miles, she'd almost forgotten all her reasons for feeling sad. She still missed her friends . . . but Madison was getting more and more excited about being in Winnetka.

"Heeeere's my driveway," Gramma pointed out as they drove onto the smooth blacktop. "Just had it paved again. Isn't that super? Do you remember coming here when you were just a pipsqueak?"

"Gramma!" Madison laughed at the old nickname. Madison nodded even though she didn't really remember much about the place.

"Well, you'll have plenty of time to get acquainted with me and my neighborhood on this trip," Gramma Helen said with a big grin.

As soon as the car stopped, Madison jumped out with Phin, who wandered around Gramma Helen's front yard, sniffing trees. He seemed to like the new surroundings. So did Madison. She glanced around for herself.

Gramma's house looked like a storybook cottage. The family had owned it for so many years—since Mom was a little girl—and Gramma claimed that it grew cozier and cozier with each year. At one time it had been reserved just as their summer house when the family moved to downtown Chicago. But now, Gramma lived by Lake Michigan all year long. She'd sold the city house long ago.

The pretty white porch was set off beautifully against the woodsy landscape, and the yard was wide open except for a jam-packed clothesline off to the side. Gramma didn't believe in clothes dryers.

Directly next to Gramma's house was another, more contemporary cottage with gigantic windows. Gramma said a family named the Millers lived there. On the opposite side was a plainer-looking house with yellow curtains and a weather vane. Her best friend, Mabel, lived there.

Around toward the back of Gramma's house was a rickety old wooden dock where Grandpa had used to moor his fishing boat.

"Let's head inside for some lunch," Gramma said when they hopped out of the car. "I'm starved."

No sooner had Madison entered the kitchen than Gramma began heating up some kind of brown stew. She had it prepared on the stove already. Madison laughed when she saw—and smelled—it. Gramma's food always smelled weird, but tasted great. She'd even set aside a goody bag of food for Phin.

Phin's nose was going crazy.

"So we'll eat and then play some cards," Gramma Helen announced. "You still good at crazy eights?"

Gramma was addicted to cards. Madison had to play three games of crazy eights before she was finally able to sneak Phin away for a short walk.

When they went out, Madison and Phinnie strolled past some of the other homes in Gramma's area. Kids were running through sprinklers on one lawn, and it reminded Madison of home. She and Aimee always cooled off that way in the summer.

What was Aimee doing right now? Madison wondered.

On the way home she bumped into Mr. Miller, the neighbor with all the windows. He introduced himself and his own dog, Cha-Cha, a terrier. Madison almost laughed out loud when she heard the dog's name. Cha-Cha and Phin seemed to "sniff" it off perfectly.

Gramma had turned on her afternoon soap operas and mystery programs by the time they returned to the house. She was sitting in the kitchen with a cup of tea, knitting blue and gold afghan squares.

"I'm making a blanket for the neighbors' new grandchild," she said, knitting one and purling two. Madison marveled at how her grandmother always kept herself busier than busy.

"So have a seat and tell me everything," Gramma said.

"Everything? Like what?" Madison asked. During their card games, she'd already filled Gramma in on the basics: school grades, friends, and even Dad.

"How are your files?" Gramma asked. "I see you brought your laptop here, so you must be keeping up with them."

Gramma always remembered to ask about the *really* important things.

Madison stood up, leaned over, and gave her a big hug and kiss. "I am so happy to be here," she said. "My files are great."

"I just want you to make yourself at home, dearie," Gramma went on. "I want this to be a great vacation. I know it's hard without your pals. . . ."

Madison sighed.

"I set up a little table in the back guest room for you and your laptop," Gramma said, winking. "So you can e-mail them."

Madison hadn't noticed it before, so she dashed into the other room to check it out. Indeed, there was a small table near a phone jack, a chair, and even a jar with pencils, pens, and a ruler. It inspired Madison to pull out her computer immediately.

"Do you mind if I try it out?" Madison asked.

"Go on, Maddie," Gramma called back. "That's what it's there for."

Madison quickly plugged in the modem and logged in to check her e-mailbox. Someone would have written by now, she thought.

But the message on-screen read otherwise.

Mailbox is empty.

Madison clicked the mail icon again. Not a single friend (or enemy) had written a note? She hadn't even received any spams or messages from unknown sources.

Mailbox is empty.

Madison had to find out what was happening. Where was everyone? Immediately she opened a new e-mail and started to type.

First she wrote to her BFFs back home.

From: MadFinn
To: BalletGrl, Wetwinz
Subject: WHERE R U GUYS???
Date: Sun 29 June 3:12 PM
_____

Where r u guys??? I am here at my
gramma's house and I MISS YOU SO
MUCH. You would like it here.
Gramma's house is on a small pond
and she has a wooden dock, but
we're only a little walk from the
big beach on Lake Michigan. So I
can go to the beach, too. Are you
spending every day at Lake Dora? I
bet ur having the best time getting
ready for the carnival and all
that, aren't you? You have to write
and send me details!

I MISS YOU!!! Did I say that
already?

p.s. Phin misses Blossom, too,
LOL

p.p.s. HB!

xoxoxxo,

Maddie

After hitting SEND, Madison typed a couple of

other e-mails to Dad, Mom, and even Egg. There was a definite theme:

WRITE!

She sent her third note in two days to Bigwheels.

```
From: MadFinn
To: Bigwheels
Subject: R U OUT THERE?
Date: Sun 29 June 3:41 PM
```
Did you get my other e-mails? R U
still in Oregon or another state? I
am FINALLY here with my gramma
Helen and my dog. I love her soooo
much. She always plans stuff for us
to do. She says she wants to teach
me how to knit. My grandmother is
so smart about things. She cooks
fun food and plays the piano and
all sorts of other stuff. You never
told me about ur grandmother. Do
you have one or two? Are they nice?

BTW: what do u do all day inside a
camper when ur driving around? Does
ur little sister get on ur nerves?
I will try to find an e-postcard
from here that will make u laugh.

Yours till the globe trotters,
MadFinn

Madison marked the entire e-mail as priority, with a red exclamation point, and then she typed an extra P.S. in big, capital letters.

P.S. WRITE BACK SOON! PRETTY PLEEZ?

Madison left bigfishbowl.com to visit her own personal files next. Without friends to chat with all the time, Madison could always talk to her files—especially when she had a lot on her mind.

 Summer Vacation

Rude Awakening: I've got a case of the summertime red, white, and blues.

Gramma says my summer visit will be a real blast, but I'm not sure. Can I have fun on the Fourth of July without my BFFs?

For a few minutes today I thought I could. Of course, being around Gramma is the best. She always is laughing. But even though Gramma is fun, I can't talk to her about boys. And Phinnie is fun, but he only speaks dog. LOL.

I did see a sign that says fireworks displays are here in Winnetka just like at home. Maybe I will have a good time—if Gramma goes with me.

What are Aimee and Fiona doing at this exact moment back in Far Hills? Aimee's probably with her Russian ballet friend Sasha buying chocolate cows at Freeze Palace. Fiona and her old BFF Debbie are probably off somewhere gabbing at the mall. Egg and Drew are at the lake, I bet. And Hart is somewhere having fun, too, still laughing about our splash fight. Hopefully he's not with Ivy.

Am I missing all the fun? It's hard to think about. So I'll try not to—as if that ever works.

After logging off again, Madison and Gramma hung out together in the living room—just talking. Madison had only been at the cottage for a few hours, but she already felt like she was at home.

"When do I get to meet Mabel?" Madison asked, looking out the window over at her neighbor's house. She was eager to meet Gramma's best friend and guessed that Mabel probably knit and played crazy eights, too. Maybe they'd have a three-way card game?

"Oh, we'll see Mabel tomorrow," Gramma said. "It's my first day with my only granddaughter! I want you all to myself right now."

Madison grinned.

"Hey, did I ever show you these?" Gramma Helen said, holding out two very fat scrapbooks that appeared to be overflowing with photographs and papers. On top of one Madison saw gold, embossed letters: FRANCINE. On the other she saw: ANGIE. One was obviously devoted to Mom. The other one was for Mom's sister, Aunt Angie.

Madison had never seen either book before, so she and Gramma sat together on the living-room sofa to take a look.

Gramma cracked the binding of Mom's book first, just as the phone rang.

"I bet that's your Mom right now," Gramma Helen said.

And it was.

Madison grabbed for the phone right away. "I love it here!" she gushed to Mom, explaining how she and Gramma Helen had shopped and played cards after leaving the airport.

But in spite of all her good cheer about Gramma's place, Madison was happier than happy to hear Mom's voice.

"I love you, honey bear," Mom said.

Madison felt like she might cry. She took a little breath. "I love you, too."

As soon as she hung up the phone, Madison settled on the couch next to Gramma Helen to finish looking at the album.

Inside FRANCINE, there were pages of baby photos and ribbons and cards. One photograph showed Mom in a baby bathing suit standing on the edge of a dock like she was getting ready to dive. She wore a little float in the shape of a giraffe.

Gramma pointed out page after page of pictures from each summer Mom had spent up at the lake house during her childhood.

"When your mom was just seven," Gramma said, turning a page, "she ran away. I thought my heart would stop. We had a neighborhood search party."

Madison giggled. From all the stories she'd always heard, Mom was good at getting herself into trouble. "So what happened?" she asked.

Gramma sighed a deep, long sigh. "Turns out she was hiding under the porch."

Madison imagined Mom on her hands and knees, hanging out with the worms and spiders under the porch. She'd changed a lot since then.

"And what's *this* picture, Gramma?" Madison pointed to a candid shot of Mom with very short hair. It spiked around her forehead.

Gramma laughed out loud. "Oh, my, that's the summer your mom's hair caught fire," she explained. "What a horror. Leaned into the stove. She cried for *weeks*. By the time she stopped crying, her old hair had practically all grown back."

Madison couldn't believe the wild things Mom had done at the lake house.

"Have you ever been fishing?" Gramma asked, turning another page. "Your grandfather used to take the kids out fishing every day of summer, I swear. See this photo here? The one with her inside the fishing boat?"

She pointed to a picture of Mom sitting in a canoe with her sister, Angie, and her father, Madison's grandpa Joe. In her hands, Mom held an enormous fish that measured almost the same size that she was.

Angie was pouting. Grandpa was posing.

Gramma caught her breath and placed her hand over the center of her chest. "Just look at the three of them," she said. "My dears."

Madison noticed that Gramma's eyes were getting a little wet.

"I miss him," Gramma said. "Your grandfather was a good man. You remind me of him sometimes, do you know that?"

Madison didn't remember much about the lake house, but she remembered lots about Grandpa Joe. It was like everything from the past blurred together a little, but he stood out. The way his scratchy beard felt when he hugged her. The way he always clicked his dentures. The way he'd play the guitar sometimes at night after they had supper. In her mind, Madison always liked to think of him as her "Pa" from *Little House on the Prairie*. He was nothing like Dad or Mom, and Grandpa Joe didn't know anything about computers, but he was that kind of superspecial that only comes along once in a while.

Zzzzzzzzzzzing!

Gramma Helen jumped into the air when the

phone rang. She leaned over the arm of the sofa and picked up the portable.

"Angie!" she said, her voice cheering right up again. "Well, I'm just sitting here with your niece, looking through some old albums. . . . Yes, we are behaving ourselves. . . . Yes, she's doing just fine. . . ."

Gramma winked at Madison.

It sounded like they'd be talking on the telephone for a while, so Madison bopped into the guest room to give Gramma some privacy.

Plus she had to see if anyone had gotten her latest e-mails.

Chapter 7

The laptop connected immediately again and her e-mailbox appeared. This time, however, Madison was in for a big surprise.

Mailbox is full.

She blinked at the screen. Full? Scrolling down, Madison was amazed to discover more than twenty e-mails. A few of them were duplicates, which seemed to have been uploaded and downloaded more than once, but there was *three* days' worth of mail here!

Right away, she deleted all the spams and advertisements, which left messages from friends and family.

Madison cruised through the rest of the list.

FROM	SUBJECT
✉ FHAS	Newsletter Update
✉ Wetwinz	Lake Party
✉ GoGramma	Your Trip
✉ TheEggMan	Computr Camp Adress
✉ Bigwheels	You Have an E-Card
✉ Dantheman	Pooches
✉ BalletGrl	Sasha's HERE!!
✉ ff_BUDGEFILM	Safe & Sound
✉ JeffFinn	Joke 4 You
✉ Sk8ingboy	Vacation
✉ BalletGrl	Re: WHERE R U GUYS???
✉ Wetwinz	Re: WHERE R U GUYS???

Some of the mail had been sent *before* Madison had left for Chicago. She realized that the bigfish bowl.com server must have been down. Whenever it crashed, the nasty server ate e-mails and then spit them back out again a day or so later.

The animal clinic had sent along its latest newsletter. Madison saved it so she could read it more closely later.

Fiona sent news about plans for meeting at Lake Dora, which had obviously already happened. Madison hit DELETE.

Gramma Helen had written with wishes for a happy journey to her house. Another DELETE. She was already here!

Then there was a doofy e-mail from Egg about his extra summer e-mail address at camp for the end of July and August. Madison saved the name to her address book just in case. Even when he was at his most irritating, Egg was still one of Madison's best friends.

Dan Ginsburg wrote about a grumpy bulldog that he and Madison liked to play with at the Far Hills clinic. Someone had adopted the dog and named her Pooches. He thought she'd want to know.

Bigwheels sent an e-card from another place in Oregon, Aimee announced the arrival of her ballet friend Sasha, Mom checked in from San Francisco, and Dad said "howdy" along with a dumb joke he had sent Madison at least twice before.

```
What do pigs put in their hard
drives? Sloppy disks! LOL

Love you, Dad
```

Madison rolled her eyes. Would Dad ever stop telling terrible jokes?

She scrolled down to the next e-mail . . . but blinked with surprise when she read the name at the top.

```
From: Sk8ingboy
```

This e-mail was from Hart Jones. *Hart Jones?* Madison pinched herself. Since Hart rarely sent her anything, she had trouble believing this was really *his* note up there on the screen. But there was no doubt. This was from the crush himself.

Even though she was still a little mad at him, Madison's heart thumped to see Hart's name flash on-screen.

```
From: Sk8ingboy
To: MadFinn
Subject: Vacation
Date: Sun 29 June 11:11 AM
Howz Chicago? Sorry about what
happened at the lake. Was that ur
hair clip? I hope so. BCNU, Hart
```

After staring numbly at the screen for a few moments longer, Madison hit SAVE. She would never delete that message.

Never.

Finally she moved on to a few of the other, more recent notes.

```
From: BalletGrl
To: MadFinn
Subject: Re: WHERE R U GUYS???
Date: Sun 29 June 5:12 PM
What r u talking about Maddie? I
have written you at least 3 emails
```

since u left! I thought u weren't
writing back to ME! Everyone MISSES
YOU SOOOOO MUCH. It is so not the
same without you here.

Sasha saw a picture of you on my
wall and she said you were
superpretty. Isn't that nice? Well,
we have a special ballet class
today so I am up early for
vacation. Then we're going to Lake
Dora again with Fiona and her
friend Debbie. Wish you were here.

Love ya,

Aim

p.s. Blossom misses Phinnie, too.

After Aimee's message, there was also a message from Fiona.

From: Wetwinz
To: MadFinn
Subject: Re: WHERE R U GUYS???
Date: Sun 29 June 5:15 PM
I have TOTALLY written back! Haven't
I? I think ur server is messed up
or something BTW. That's why u
couldn't get mail.

OF COURSE WE MISS U!

Life here is square. My brother,
Chet, is being a loser, but Egg
has been over visiting a lot this
weekend, so he and I have been
hanging out. Don't SAY IT! You know
what I mean. I can't help liking
Egg even if he is a weirdo.
Besides, I am one too. :>)

My friend Debbie sez hello 2 you.
She's different than I remember
from home though. She is a little
stuck up or something. More on
that l8r.

Sooooo you have 2 send news about
ur Gramma's house. Does she have a
scanner? Can u send a picture of
you and Phin? I can put it up like
a screen saver while u r away. BYE
FOR NOW!

xoxoxoxxoxox Fiona

Madison was just about to write to Bigwheels yet
again when Gramma interrupted with a boom.
    "Maddie!" she wailed from the other room.
"Come get supper!"
    It was already way after six o'clock. As usual,

dinner smelled funny but tasted yummy. Only Gramma Helen could make a grilled cheese sandwich taste so good. And after the table was cleared off, Madison and Gramma played more games of crazy eights until almost ten o'clock. Madison was sure that after a week in Winnetka, *she'd* be addicted to card playing, too.

With bedtime approaching, the dishes washed, and the cards (finally) put away, Gramma sent Madison out to the front curb with one last task: taking out the bag of garbage. She said it was nice to have a helping hand around to lift the heavy things.

"Just drop it in the brown barrel, okay?" Gramma said. "The green container is Mabel's."

Madison hoisted the garbage over one shoulder and pushed open the screen door. All she could hear was crickets. All she could see was pale moonlight. She walked with the garbage to the end of the path and slowly lifted the brown lid.

But Madison wasn't alone out there.

Out of the corner of her eye, she saw a flicker . . . and then another person.

A boy was standing next to her, hands on the green barrel. *Mabel's barrel.*

The boy called out, "Whassup?" Then he tossed in his trash before disappearing without another word.

Madison rushed back inside.

"Who is that boy next door?" she squealed to

Gramma Helen when she came back in. "You didn't tell me your friend Mabel had a grandson!"

"Oh, you must have seen Mark," Gramma said. "Silly me! I forgot that he'd be visiting this week. Guess I was just so excited to have you here all to myself that I forgot. . . ."

"How could you forget?" Madison asked. "Gramma, there is a cute boy next door. How could you forget *that*?"

Gramma chuckled. "He is cute, isn't he?"

"How old is he? Where is he from?" Madison asked. "Is he nice?"

"One question at a time! Let's see. . . . I think he's around fourteen. And his parents live right here in Chicago. He comes to visit quite often, actually. I thought he was coming *next* week. Must have gotten the dates swapped."

Madison rushed over to the living room windows on the side of the house that directly faced Mabel's house. She tugged back the curtain just a little bit and saw that there were still lights on next door. She could make out people moving inside the living room.

"Maddie! What are you doing?" Gramma asked.

Madison shut the curtains gently. "Oh. I was just looking . . ."

"Looking?" Gramma crossed her arms.

Madison knew she was turning three shades of violet. "For Mark," she admitted. "I wanted to see what he looked like if I could. . . . He seemed cute, but it was pretty dark out there . . . and . . ."

The strange new boy had left Madison tongue-tied.

"Maddie, I'm sure Mabel would love to introduce you to her grandson," Gramma said. "Why don't we meet up with them tomorrow, as I said?"

"Really?" Madison gulped. "Oh no, that would be way too embarrassing. . . ."

"Nonsense!" Gramma said. "That's exactly what we need to do. I'll call Mabel first thing."

Gramma plopped down onto the sofa and Phinnie jumped up and danced around her. He wanted his back rubbed. She leaned over to scratch.

On the other side of the room, Madison yawned and collapsed into an upholstered chair. It was odd to feel her heart racing so fast inside such a tired body.

"Let's get to bed," Gramma said. "We have a big day tomorrow . . . and now, apparently, it's going to be even bigger."

Madison nodded with a smile. "Yeah."

She went to get herself ready for bed.

Lying there on top of the covers in her favorite Lisa Simpson nightshirt, Madison watched as bright moonlight cast shadows across her bed and walls. A giant fan in the window hummed while it sucked all the hot air out of the room.

Phinnie snuggled closer to Madison. Although his

fur made her legs twitch, Madison was too preoccupied to let it bother her.

She closed her eyes again and thought about what it would be like to *really* meet the boy next door.

She'd be finding out soon enough.

Chapter 8

By the time the next morning rolled around, Madison had mapped out how, when, and where she'd meet Mark. She even imagined what she'd say.

The only trouble spot was figuring out what to *wear*.

"Holy cow!" Gramma cried as she wandered into the guest room. "Did a cyclone pass through here?"

"No, Gramma," Madison said. "I just don't know what would look good." She'd tossed the entire contents of her suitcase onto the floor and across her unmade bed.

"What's wrong with what you have on?" Gramma asked, surveying Madison's outfit: a yellow tank top with a smile face, faded jean shorts, and sneakers.

"Ick!" Madison said, looking into the mirror on the wall. "Ick! Ick! Ick! This color looks bad. I feel uncomfortable in these shorts. . . ." She tugged at the legs and pulled them right off.

Gramma sat down quietly on the edge of the bed and started to fold up some of the clothes strewn nearby. Madison pulled on a new pair of green cargo shorts that Mom had bought on sale at the mall. They felt better than the jeans.

"For goodness' sake, Maddie, we're only going into town to run a few errands. We'll be back before lunch," Gramma said. "And I think you look fine."

Madison glanced over at the mirror once again. There was only one thing missing. She dumped out her plastic bag of little shampoos and barrettes onto the bed and located her brand-new tube of strawberry-kiwi lip gloss, smacking some onto her lips with a smile. She offered Gramma some gloss, too.

"Oh," Gramma said coyly. "Not for me!" But Madison insisted.

Soon enough her grandmother had smacking strawberry-kiwi lips just like Madison's. Phin got water and some kibble, and Madison and Gramma Helen went shopping.

First they stopped by a stationery store, the dry cleaners, and Radio Zone, an electronics outlet. The only people they ran into were shop owners Gramma knew and one friend who lived in her neighborhood, a sweet old man named Fred. Madison was certain they'd run into Mabel and Mark on the street somewhere . . . but they didn't.

She looked for them in car window reflections, on the sidewalk, and even at the bank line. But they weren't anywhere in the village of Winnetka.

Gramma drove a scenic route on the way home, pointing out the big mansions and smaller cottages along the lake where her friends lived. Some had picket fences painted yellow. Others had giant, in-ground swimming pools. Folks on bicycles sped past them, and Gramma waved at everyone.

By the time they arrived home, Madison was actually starting to forget about Mark, or at least trying to forget.

And then she saw him—in daylight. Standing on the newly paved driveway.

Looking cuter than cute.

"Well, I'll be!" Gramma said, smiling, as she pulled in her car. She rolled down her window. "Hello, there, Mark!"

Mark smiled back. "Hello, Mrs. Hirsh!"

Madison could feel her body sticking to the car seat.

"I'd like you to meet my granddaughter, Madison," Gramma said, pulling the car up next to Mark. He gave Maddie a high sign but didn't say much more.

Neither did she.

"My grandmother was trying to call you," Mark said to Gramma Helen. "Your answering machine isn't working, she said."

"Oh, dear," Gramma said. "I've been meaning to get that thing fixed. Well, you tell Mabel we'll be over later, okay?"

Madison was sinking into the hot front seat. She wanted to run, but there was nowhere to go. She couldn't believe that she was wearing her yellow tank top—and all her lip gloss had been chewed off. She knew she should have changed shirts! And what did her hair look like?

"Okay, then," Mark said to Gramma Helen, quickly turning back toward Mabel's cottage. "See you later!"

Madison turned to the side to avoid looking in his direction. She shifted in her seat so her legs wouldn't stick.

Why did this boy make her so nervous?

She'd hoped for a very different first meeting.

After they unloaded the car, Madison got Phin for his midday walk. Gramma suggested that they take another scenic route, down the road toward Tower Head Beach. It was close by, and Phin could have fun in the sand. Dogs were allowed on this beach.

"Maybe you'll make a doggy friend down there," Gramma cooed at Phin. He panted back at her.

"I'll be right back," Madison said.

"Take your time, Maddie!" Gramma cried. "We'll go visit Mabel and Mark when you get back."

Madison's pulse raced. All she could think about

was running into Mark again in the same yellow shirt she had on now. Frantically she handed Phin's leash over to Gramma, ran into the guest room, and quickly changed into a new pink shirt with a little daisy on it. *Just in case.*

Gramma shook her head. "You look FINE!" she said for the tenth time. "Now, give me a big smooch good-bye and skedaddle!"

It only took Madison and Phin ten minutes to find the beach. Madison saw people gathered together by a row of shiny blue and red bicycles near a sandy path. There was a giant sign over a parking lot entrance that read TOWER HEAD BEACH. Several soggy-looking kids, who looked like they had been hanging out all day in Lake Michigan, tossed a Frisbee around. There was a concession stand, showers, and even a sandbox and playground.

Many of the kids Madison saw were younger than she was, more like eight and nine, not twelve and thirteen. There were families and teenagers and grandparents everywhere. Everyone seemed to know each other, lingering by the bluffs and crowded around picnic tables. Madison guessed that Gramma came here often. She probably carted her watercolor paint set and easel down to the shore to spend afternoons, painting children and waves.

She probably knew everyone *here*, too.

Over to one side, Madison noticed a girl staring in her direction. They seemed to be about the same age. A moment later, the girl approached. She wore a bathing suit with a flower in the center, just like Madison's suit.

"Hey," she said. "Cute dog." She leaned over to pet Phin.

Phin gave the girl a happy snort in return.

"Hi," Madison replied. "I'm Madison. This is Phin."

The girl introduced herself as Pam. "Do you live here?" she asked.

"Oh no, I'm just visiting. Visiting my grandmother," Madison said. "What about you?"

"Just visiting," Pam said. "How long are you here?"

"A week. I came for the Fourth of July," Madison said. She wondered if maybe Pam was the antidote for BFF withdrawal. They could go to the celebration together.

"Oh, that Fourth of July thing sounds like fun. There's supposed to be this awesome fireworks display in downtown Winnetka," Pam said.

"Sounds great," Madison said. "Are you going?"

"Not me." Pam shook her head. "I'm actually leaving tomorrow."

"Leaving?" Madison said.

Her stomach was sinking . . . sinking . . . SUNK.

"Bummer," Madison added, trying to paste on a fake smile.

"Yeah, I really want to go home for the Fourth of

July," Pam said. "And see my BFFs, you know? I'd rather hang with them than . . . well, than with my grandpa and grandma. You know? Even though the lake is cool and all that . . ."

Madison nodded. "Yeah, well . . ."

Of course she knew. *Exactly.*

"Well, I gotta go. It was nice to meet you. Bye, Phin!" Pam said before dashing away. She hopped on a bike and took off through one parking lot.

Madison waved.

How had she made and lost a friend in less than five minutes?

It was some kind of new world record.

She and Phin turned around toward home. Gramma Helen was just the person to cheer Madison up all over again.

When she got back to the house, however, Gramma was on her way out the door.

"Where are you going?" Madison asked.

"Oh, hello!" Gramma said. "I left you a note on the counter. Mabel invited us over for tea. Isn't that nice?"

Madison panicked. "Tea?" she said. She wanted to meet Mabel. But she was too nervous to meet Mark.

"Shake a leg! Let's go!" Gramma said. "We can bring Phin, too."

"Well . . ." Madison stalled. "The truth is, Gramma, that I'm not feeling that well. Maybe it was

90

the walk to the beach. I'm just a little hot, and my stomach . . . kind of . . . *aches.*"

Gramma reached out and felt Madison's head. "You're sick? You don't feel feverish."

"I just don't know if I'm up to meeting someone. . . ." Madison continued. She coughed a little for effect.

"Maddie, Mabel would really love to meet you!" Gramma said. She tried to convince Madison of the 101 reasons why she should go.

But Madison moaned and groaned and got her way.

She'd stay put.

"Well," Gramma said reluctantly. "If you change your mind, we're right next door. And when I come back, we'll find something to do that doesn't make you so . . . achy."

The way Gramma said that, Madison wondered if Gramma knew she might be faking.

Moments after she left, Madison spied on Gramma and Mabel through the living-room curtains. They sat down around a table at the kitchen next door, pouring cups of tea and laughing.

Mark wasn't around, but Madison scrunched down into the sofa just to make doubly sure that neither he—nor anyone—would see her there.

Phinnie jumped up on the sofa, panting. He had been frisky since they'd gotten back from the beach, and he still had some sand in his little pug paws.

Madison petted his head and told him to calm down, but he wouldn't. He jumped off the sofa and then jumped right back on again. He leaped up so fast that his paw caught the edge of the curtain and nearly dragged it down off its rod.

Madison fell into the window with a smack but quickly recovered. She shooed Phin off the sofa and peeked out the window again.

But no one was in the kitchen anymore.

Brrrrrring!

Phin howled when the doorbell rang. Madison thought her heart had stopped. But she also knew who she would discover on the welcome mat.

Gramma and Mabel.

Mabel was all smiles. "Ooooooh!" she cooed, grabbing Madison's cheeks. "You're twice as pretty as your picture!"

Gramma was beaming, too. "Isn't she?"

Madison cringed with all the attention. She felt like she was a toddler—not an almost teenager. Mabel's hands were cold, too, and she smelled like bread.

"How's the tummy?" Gramma Helen asked as they walked inside. "We were going to leave you alone, but Mabel just couldn't wait to meet you. Are you feeling any better now that you sat down for a while?"

Madison cocked her head from side to side. "I guess so," she mumbled, rubbing her abdomen for effect.

"You look a little pale," Mabel said, reaching for Madison's forehead, just like Gramma had done earlier.

As Madison leaned to shut the front door behind them, Mark unexpectedly appeared on the stoop.

"Hey!" he said. "I just ran back to get my grandmother's cane. She left it in the hall. Can I come in?"

Madison glanced down and saw that Mabel had an Ace bandage wrapped tightly around her ankle.

"Well, yeah," Madison said. Mark was even cuter than when she'd seen him in the driveway. She was trying not to stare but wasn't having much luck.

"Grams!" Mark called out as he walked inside. Mabel turned around when she heard Mark's voice, and then everyone went into the other room.

Madison rocked from heel to toe, heel to toe. She couldn't stand still.

Why did this boy make her so nervous?

Everyone sat together in the living room. Gramma and Mabel started gossiping about their other neighbor, Mr. Miller.

Mark looked bored. He turned to Madison. "Are you here for the rest of the summer?" he asked.

"Uh-huh," Madison said, still staring. She barely could get the words out. "Wait! I mean, no. I mean . . . I'm only here for a week. Duh. I don't know why I said that."

Mark laughed. "I came to help my grandmother.

She's been kind of sick, you know? But she's getting better now."

"I saw her limping," Madison said.

"Yeah, she fell last week and sprained her ankle. My mother and I drove over here to help. I stayed," Mark said.

"Where do you live?" Madison asked. Her lip twitched nervously the way it sometimes did around Hart—only *more* so.

"Me and my sister and parents live in Chicago," Mark explained. "It's only twenty miles away. Where do you live?"

"New York," Madison said.

"New York *City*?" Mark asked, his voice rising excitedly.

"Nearby," Madison said. "I live in a town called Far Hills. It's a train ride into the city."

"Oh," Mark said. "Cool."

He fell silent. The air was thick as mashed potatoes between them. Gramma and Mabel were still gabbing between themselves about the weather.

"So . . ." Madison said.

"So . . ." Mark said.

Phinnie ran over and leaped onto Mark. He started jumping up and down, and Mark cracked up. Madison cringed with more embarrassment. First it was her ugly shirt, and now it was her silly dog!

"Phinnie!" Madison cried, trying to pull him down.

"He's okay," Mark reassured her. "I love dogs. In fact, I saw you walking him yesterday."

"I think I saw you out at the trash cans, too," Madison said.

"Yeah, that was me," he admitted.

Madison smiled. For some reason, Mark was slowly taking away all of her nervousness. She asked him questions about school and his grandmother and what he liked to do for fun. He answered quickly and asked the same questions right back. He seemed as curious about her as she was about him.

"So you're only here for a week," Mark said.

"Yep," she said.

"Too bad I'm leaving soon," Mark said.

"Leaving? You *are*?" Madison asked with disbelief. Was he going to be just like Pam, the nice girl from Tower Head Beach, heading somewhere better and bigger for the upcoming festivities?

"I'm taking off this week," he said.

Madison caught her breath.

"But you'll be here for the Fourth of July?" Madison asked.

"Oh yeah!" Mark said. "I wouldn't miss THAT. No way. I like to go down to the Village Commons after the parade. They have this awesome Winnetka barbecue, and free sparklers, and the best carnival. Better than the one near us in Chicago. I would NEVER miss this."

Madison's stomach flip-flopped. "It does sound

95

like fun," she said, her voice drifting off. "I should go. . . ."

"Yeah, well . . ." he said. "Anyway . . ."

"Anyway . . ." Madison said.

"See you around?" he said.

"I guess so," Madison replied, not sure if he'd been asking a real question or just saying good-bye.

"Yeah," Mark continued. "Maybe we could do something with our grandmothers. Or there's Tower Beach or tennis. Or whatever."

"Sure," Madison said. "SURE!"

She caught herself staring again.

How could Madison already be feeling the fireworks . . . when it wasn't even July Fourth yet?

Chapter 9

On Tuesday morning, Gramma pulled Madison out of bed just as the sun was about to come up.

"Let's go watch the sky turn colors as the sun rises," Gramma told Madison, who could barely keep her eyes open.

"It's too early." Madison yawned. "Gramma!"

"Nonsense!" Gramma exclaimed. "When the light changes, the water changes color, too. Lake Michigan is filled with life. Come on!"

In addition to painting the sunrise, Gramma explained, she wanted to take Madison for a little bird watching. There was too much to do!

Madison rubbed her eyes and grabbed the binoculars. "I think I'm going to fall asleep standing up," she told Gramma.

But of course she didn't.

Madison put on Phinnie's leash, and they piled into the car and drove toward Tower Head Beach.

A few more yawns later, everything magically changed. Madison became alert, gabbing with Gramma as they parked the car and walked down to the dunes. The beach was practically empty.

"Stick with me," Gramma said. "I'll show you where the fun is."

Madison laughed. She tried to imagine Aimee and Egg and the rest of the Far Hills group getting up at the crack of dawn to look at birds and sand.

Twee-leet! Twee-leet!

Madison whirled her head around and looked into the air for the bird making that noise. Gramma pointed to a red-winged bird on a pine tree branch high above the beach. Then they saw a yellow-bellied bird fly by.

Koo-koo cheeeeeep!

Gramma took out a fold-up stool, a sketch pad, and watercolors, then sat down, and started to paint the tree and the birds. Madison watched her grandmother's paintbrush move gently over the paper. Gramma could do anything. The birds came to life in pale colors on the page. And Lake Michigan shimmered as the sun rose up in the distance, just as Gramma said it would.

Sitting together on the sand, Madison guessed that this was one of the "summer surprises" Mom had talked about. By the time the sun had fully risen, Madison helped Gramma pack up her things again and reload the car.

"Let's go get breakfast," Gramma said. "I made cranberry muffins. Do you like those?"

Madison nodded even though she'd never tried them before. But if Gramma made them, she knew they'd be good.

While the muffins toasted and the hot chocolate heated, Madison and Gramma played a round of crazy eights on Madison's request. She liked the card game more and more—mostly because it was Gramma's favorite.

She liked everything about her stay in Winnetka so far. Even if the boy next door made her nervous, Madison had Gramma to make everything better.

Since they'd gotten up so early, it seemed like the whole day had gone by when it was only noontime! After breakfast, Madison and Gramma looked through more photo albums and reminisced some more about what Mom was like as a kid. Every story was like a piece of candy that Gramma unwrapped and fed to Madison.

When the funny cuckoo clock in Gramma's living room struck twelve, Madison peered through the curtains again to see if Mark or Mabel would appear. They didn't. And Mabel's car wasn't in the driveway, either.

Gramma went back to her knitting in the afternoon. She didn't want to sit outside when the sun was hottest because she said her head fried like an egg in the sun. Gramma was always coming up with expressions like that. Plus if she knit for an hour or so, that meant Madison would have extra time on her laptop.

Although she loved hanging out with Gramma all day, Madison was grateful for the time alone. She still owed Bigwheels another e-mail—and she wanted to see if Aimee or Fiona had written again.

She logged on and started writing.

From: MadFinn
To: Bigwheels
Subject: I am in LIKE
Date: Tues 1 July 12:34 PM
How are u? How is your camper? Are you meeting any new friends while camping? I think it is so fun that you and my mom are right now in the exact same location in the USA. She's in California now, too, did I tell you that? Where are you going next? I got your last e-card. Thanks for that. I still need to send you one, but I haven't seen any here in Winnetka. My gramma drew this cool picture of birds

this morning, though. Maybe I'll
send that.

I have sort of big vacation news I
am dying to tell you. There is this
boy who lives next door to Gramma
(well, he's just visiting next
door), and I think I am in total
like even though we only met a day
ago (well, really we just talked
yesterday for the first time). I
know this is totally wacky because
I like that guy Hart from my
school, right? This guy's name is
Mark, and he has brown hair, too,
just like Hart, but he doesn't act
all goofy like Hart does. He's a
little older too, he's 14, but it
doesn't really matter except he
seems a little more mature.

Maybe instead of an e-card, I'll
send a picture of me and Mark!
Yeah, right!

Yours till the sun tans,

MadFinn, aka Maddie

p.s. I am attaching this cool
survey that someone sent to me

online. Please fill it out and send
me a copy back. Then send it on to
your other friends. I' ll send one
to you, too, later.

<Attachment: whatrulike.doc>

**Madison zoomed out of the e-mailbox and
double-checked her buddy list. Aimee and Fiona
were both online, so she sent off an Insta-
Message . . . instantly.**

Hey what r u doing online NOW?
Meet me in private chat room
    MISSYOU

She had to wait awhile for her BFFs to respond.

<Wetwinz>: Maddie?
<MadFinn>: FIONA!
<BalletGrl>: Maddie?
<MadFinn>: How r u guys? What' s
    gnu?
<BalletGrl>: WE MISS YOU and I have
    a sunburn ouch
<Wetwinz>: it has been soooo hot
    here we' ve been @ the lake like
    EVRY DAY
<BalletGrl>: Sasha and Debbie wish
    they could meet u, it' s not the
    same summer w/o YOU

```
<MadFinn>: I'm ok here—I made a new
    friend
<BalletGrl>: 8-]
<Wetwinz>: kool whats her name
```

**Madison was about to type, *He's a BOY friend!*
but she stopped herself and changed the subject.**

```
<MadFinn>: SO how's Egg, Fiona?
<Wetwinz>: GR8
<BalletGrl>: He asked her to go to
    the Fourth of July!!
<MadFinn>: WDYS?
<Wetwinz>: :>) he did :>)
<BalletGrl>: I'm going with them but
    still . . .
<MadFinn>: what about Ben?
<BalletGrl>: Maddie quit it!
<MadFinn>: YYSSW
<Wetwinz>: :>) ur funny
<BalletGrl>: Next subject pleez
<Wetwinz>: my friend Debbie has a
    bf (boyfriend)
<BalletGrl>: Yeah and Sasha is
    wicked experienced too w/boys—she
    has done a lot I was surprised
    when she told me
<MadFinn>: wow so what else
<Wetwinz>: well, we heard wicked
    gossip
<MadFinn>: what?
```

```
<BalletGrl>: it's no big deal—they
   deserve each other anyhow
<MadFinn>: WHAT?
<Wetwinz>: Ivy and Hart r going to
   the fireworks party 2gether on
   July 4—Egg told me
```

Madison paused at the keyboard. She felt a little lump in her throat.

```
<BalletGrl>: Hello? Maddie? R u
   there?
<MadFinn>: Y I'm here
<BalletGrl>: I know you don't
   care about stupid Ivy, but ur
   friends w/Hart right? He would
   listen 2 u. Couldn't you tell
   him that he CANNOT date the
   enemy?
<Wetwinz>: wait chet told me that
   Hart really likes her though—I
   think he'll go
```

Madison's fingers stopped typing right there in the middle of the e-conversation. How could he have sent *her* that nice e-mail and then . . . planned a date with Ivy? She pictured the two of them sitting together on a rock on a beach somewhere, holding hands. She wanted to cry.

Ivy always got what she wanted.

```
<BalletGrl>: N e way, no biggie.
   Maddie?
<Wetwinz>: helloooooooooooooooo?
<MadFinn>: yeah Im here but I have
   to go now sorry
<Wetwinz>: okay TTYL
<BalletGrl>: I MISS YOU!
<MadFinn>: *poof*
```

For the first time since she'd landed at the airport, Madison felt a little homesick. Her head was woozy, too, spinning with thoughts of Hart and Ivy . . . and Ivy and Hart . . . and . . .

Was this gossip true?

"Maddie?" Gramma Helen poked her head into the guest room, where Maddie was sitting, only to catch her granddaughter staring at a blank computer screen. "Is everything okay in here?" she asked.

Madison sighed. "Not really."

Gramma scooted over to Madison's bedside. "Well, cheer up. You have a visitor," she said softly. "At the front door."

"Huh?" Madison said. "A visitor?" A moment later, it hit her. Who else would be visiting her here? *Mark.*

"He's here?" Madison said, her voice squeaking a little. "HERE?"

"Shhh. Yes, he's in the living room, and I said I'd

come get you. I think he might want to go to the beach. He's got a towel with him. Do you want to go to the beach again? It's not too late in the day, and you could go swimming. He is *such* a nice boy."

Madison jumped out of her chair and peered through the crack in the door. Mark was indeed sitting on the living room sofa, bag and towel by his feet, cracking his knuckles.

"Oh no," Madison whispered. "What am I supposed to do now?"

Gramma grinned. "You're supposed to go."

Phinnie barked as if to say, "WOOF! GO!"

And so five minutes later, Madison was headed out the door in her flowered bathing suit and blue T-shirt, swimming towel, and flip-flops.

Madison couldn't believe how crowded Tower Head Beach was when they arrived on the scene sometime after two-thirty. She and Mark walked over together, gabbing about gulls and sand and other beach stuff. He knew some fun trivia about Lake Michigan that made Madison laugh.

They threw their towels on the sand. Mark suggested they go in for a quick swim right away. Madison tugged the edges of her blue T-shirt. She didn't feel like dashing into the water like him. She dug her heel into the sand.

"The water here is warm in summer," Mark said, running for the edge. "Come on! Don't worry!"

Madison watched Mark dodge a few kids and dive into a shallow wave.

Without even thinking, she pulled off her T-shirt and followed in after him. A few moments later, Madison was standing there, waist high in Lake Michigan, in nothing more than a bathing suit. For most people, this would not have been a huge deal, but for Madison Finn, it was a MEGA-huge deal.

Splash! Sploosh!

Madison squinted up into the sun. Mark had splashed fistfuls of water in her direction, and she had to blink to see clearly. Luckily it was fresh water and not salty like the ocean.

"Cut it out!" Madison giggled. She wiped her face and dunked down into the water so she'd be all wet.

Splash! Sploosh!

Mark kept right on splashing.

"You better watch out!" Madison yelled, splashing back. A seagull squawked as it passed overhead, and for a moment, Madison wished she'd brought Phinnie so he could swim, too.

Splash! Sploosh!

Unlike back at Lake Dora, Madison was *enjoying* this splash feud. She splashed Mark and nearly knocked him over.

"Hey," Mark cried. "No fair!"

Madison laughed and ran out of the water toward her towel. The lake was getting a little cooler now. She slipped on her blue T-shirt and wrapped her towel tight around her shoulders.

"That was fun," she said as Mark approached his own towel and sat down on the beach. He agreed.

"We should play tennis, too," he said. "Can you play?"

Madison nodded. "Sort of. I can hit the ball back a little bit. I almost went to tennis camp one summer."

She and Mark sat together in silence and waited for the sun to dry them off a little more. Then they walked back toward their grandmothers' houses.

Mark walked Madison to the door of Gramma Helen's cottage. She felt the same surge of nerves she'd felt the night near the garbage cans.

"See you later, then," he said, walking backward away from Madison.

Madison smiled. "Maybe see you tomorrow?" she said, not believing that she'd actually asked him that question. It was bolder than she'd *ever* been with Hart.

But Mark made a face. "Aw, I can't tomorrow morning. I have to go with my grandmother to the clinic. For her ankle, you know? Sorry."

"Oh," Madison said. "Okay."

"Maybe when I get back?" he asked. "I'd love to hang out with your dog or something."

Madison wrinkled her brows.

Hang out with the dog?

"Oh," Madison said again. "Okay."

Mark turned and walked away without saying another word. He just raised his hand up with a good-bye wave.

Madison waved, too.

And the moment she walked inside the front entryway at Gramma Helen's house, she ran to find Phin.

"Oh, Phinnieeeee!" she said, letting out a little scream of glee.

Phinnie nearly fell off the sofa.

Chapter 10

On Wednesday afternoon, all plans were off. It poured.

Gramma even decided to stop playing cards because her back was aching, so she lay down for a long nap.

Madison had to find something else to keep herself occupied.

Mark wasn't around, so she couldn't hang out with him.

And Phinnie was useless company. That dog just wanted to sleep next to Gramma's dishwasher.

After trying in vain to get any reception on Gramma's broken-down TV set, Madison attempted to piece together one of the thirty or so puzzles that had been collecting dust over the years on Gramma's basement shelves. She found piles of puzzles featuring gum ball jars, cityscapes, and beach scenes, finally settling on a puzzle called Big Sky. But after only fifteen minutes, Madison even gave up on that. She was lost in all those blue clouds.

Ultimately, Madison turned to her laptop for companionship. She curled into the big, upholstered living room chair and settled in to work on her files.

Rain

How could yesterday be so perfect and today is like massive cloud cover—over my whole LIFE? Okay, I'm exaggerating a little. But because of the stupid rain, I sat here all morning inside with Gramma going crazy playing crazy eights. And I didn't meet up with Mark, who I really, REALLY wanted to see today. And now I'm just alone.

Rude awakening: Is there an umbrella to keep people from raining on my parade?

Bigwheels says that rain is the best thing in the whole world. She told me once that she loves raindrops on her face and her hair. But I don't get it. Rain makes ME grumpier than grumpy.

I wonder if Mark likes the rain?

Mark, Mark, Mark.

Why can't I get him out of my mind?

As she sat there writing, Madison had to admit that the sound of raindrops on windows was rather comforting. Warm, summer rainfall plinking on the house was like a kind of music all around. And there was no lightning or thunder that raged with this storm, just a steady stream of gray and wet running down the glass, down the street, and down the downspout.

Just thinking about Mark in the rain made Madison smile. She secretly wished he were around so she could run away to the beach with him (even if they got drenched) or play some kind of rain-splashing game together. But Mark and Mabel probably wouldn't be returning to Winnetka Village until late.

As the afternoon—and Gramma's nap—went on, Madison alternated between writing and reading in the big chair. Two more file updates and four more chapters into her book later, she finally moved—because she had to move.

Phin needed a walk.

"ROWRROOOOO!"

If she hated rain, her dog hated it *twice* as much. Phinnie howled and scowled and pulled backward on his leash so Madison couldn't even get him out the door at first. And even when he did make it out-doors, the pug protested by not peeing. He sat his little bottom right down in the mud and refused to budge.

"Phinnie!" Madison shrieked at the dog. "Get UP!"

"Rowrorooooo!" Phin barked again. He wasn't moving anywhere.

When she realized the dog was being more stubborn than she was, Madison started to drag Phin across the lawn. He yelped a little but finally followed her obediently. Madison leaned over a few times to rub his wet paws and check to make sure that he wasn't getting too cold and damp. Phin snorted in continued protest but finally did what he was supposed to do and then scrambled for the porch at Gramma's house. Madison opened the door and he wiggled inside, curly tail going as fast as it could.

Gramma was finally up from her nap by the time the pair returned.

"You two are soaked to the skin!" she said.

Madison shrugged her wet shoulders. "I guess so. Why does it have to rain so much, Gramma?"

Throwing a towel around Madison's back, Gramma squeezed. "It's good, all this rain. Good for the flowers. Good for the skin. Good for *you* . . ."

Madison sighed. Gramma *was* good at saying wise things, but even those words didn't soothe Madison's grumpy disposition.

"I have an idea," Gramma suggested, trying to change the mood. "Why don't you go out to the backyard? In the shed out there, I've got some watercolor paint kits. We could paint and make some art together. Maybe you could even make one of those collages you're so good at doing."

It sounded way better than any ideas Madison had, so she obliged.

"Don't get all drenched again!" Gramma warned, but of course it was too late. Once again, Madison faced the spitting rain. She was soaked in seconds.

Inside the shed was a row of shelves piled high with junk, junk, and more junk. Lots of stuff was left over from the days of Grandpa Joe. This shed had been his special place, with special objects shoved into every available space: motors that didn't work, rusted tools, coffee tins of bolts and screws, buckets of fishhooks and wire, three old rods and reels, and even a tacked-up calendar with a red racing car on the front.

Madison's eyes pored over the calendar, open to the month that Grandpa had died. He'd marked something in almost every little square. Madison focused on one square in particular, reading Grandpa's scribbled handwriting:

Maddie's birthday—send birdhouse

She remembered that day clearly. He'd sent a yellow-painted house that still hung in the largest tree in her Far Hills backyard.

Her eyes searched the wall for other memories.

Near the calendar, Madison noticed a faded photograph thumbtacked onto the wall. In the picture, Grandpa Joe and Gramma Helen and Mom and Aunt Angie were posing together at the beach—it looked

114

like Tower Head Beach—when they were much younger. Mom had curly hair. Angie was pulling on her hand. Everyone was smiling.

Way up in a corner, near some rafters, Madison caught a glimmer of something else, too. Words had been carved into the wood on the side of the shed. Intrigued, she looked around everywhere for a light to read the words by.

She finally found a neon-colored flashlight—on a set of metal shelves across the room—and it worked! Madison grabbed it, crawled up onto a worktable, and tried to get a closer look at the carving.

FRAN ❤ ETHAN

Madison gulped and looked closer.
Had Mom really written this?
In smaller letters nearby, Madison also saw yet another jagged carving. This one was harder to read, but Madison recognized that it had been scrawled by the same person.

F + E 4-EVER

Madison grinned. Mom *had* written both of these.

All at once, it was like her mother was right there in the shed, too. Madison could hear Mom's voice, laughing, like she had on the airplane, telling the story about her own childhood loves. Mom had been in love right here in this very spot.

Between the old photos and objects and the sound of rain still beating on the shed roof, Madison got a case of the shivers. All her feelings were stuck in her throat. Mom had been so right. The past was sleeping everywhere inside the shed. This place *was* magical.

Madison crawled back down off the rickety table and replaced the flashlight on one of the metal shelves. There she also saw the watercolor paint sets Gramma asked about and grabbed them along with a box with paper, brushes, and cups. Carting the paints back inside the main house, Madison suddenly felt her entire mood shift.

Phinnie was jumping up and down and in circles when Madison came back into the dry living room. He barked and sniffed her all over.

"You found everything okay?" Gramma asked when her granddaughter reappeared.

Madison nodded and heaved the box of paints onto the kitchen table. They pored over the materials together for several minutes and set up a mini-studio right there in the kitchen.

"I think I'm going to make a card for Mark," Madison said coyly. She smiled as she pulled on one of Gramma's funny painting smocks.

"Ooooooh!" Gramma said. "What a fine idea."

Gramma helped Madison find some old magazines and scissors and glue, too. This would be one of her fine collage masterpieces, Madison decided. She flipped through magazines for all the right words and phrases.

Summer in the City
Go for a swim!
What a blast . . .

"You don't think this is dumb, do you?" Madison asked Gramma. "I mean, I only just met him. Do you think he'll think I'm a weirdo for making him a card? Do boys even like cards?"

Gramma nodded. "He'll appreciate it, Maddie, I know it. Mark is a fine young man. And I'm sure he likes you, too."

"I never said I LIKED him," Madison squealed.

"Oh," Gramma corrected herself. "I guess I misunderstood."

"Yeah," Madison said. "We're just friends, and not even good ones. We only just met, right?"

Gramma kept right on nodding. "Right. Of course."

They painted and pasted for almost two hours, without saying much more about Mark. When Madison showed Gramma the card, she said it looked perfect. Collage words covered the front. Inside, Madison had painted a picture of the beach with the words *Summer Vacation* and signed it, *Thanks for showing me around, Madison Finn.*

While the card was sitting out on the table

drying, Madison peered through the living room curtains to see if anyone had come back home from Winnetka Village yet. She was surprised to see lights on next door—and shadows, too.

Mark and Mabel were home.

But by now, it was dinnertime and too late to go knocking on Mark's door and bring over the card. She'd have to hand-deliver it some other time.

Gramma whipped up some macaroni for dinner while Madison got distracted once again by her laptop computer files. As usual, her brain was buzzing with ideas and emotions. She had to write them all down.

Drowning

When I asked the Ask the Blowfish back home (on bigfishbowl.com) about what would happen on this part of my summer vacation, the fortune-teller fish told me I would be drowning in a sea of love.

HA HA HA. That's a joke.

Rude awakening: With all this rain, I sure am drowning—but in the "we'll see" of love.

Mark has been gone all day. Was that for the best? The Fourth of July is only 2 days away and I doubt that I'll go with him. I shouldn't get my hopes up, right? Plus I think that I should spend the holiday with Gramma Helen instead. She would be sooo sad if I didn't.

And I can't forget about Hart, either.
How can I like two people at once? It's
hard to figure all this out, especially
when I'm so far from home.

"Maddie!" Gramma Helen's voice echoed
throughout the house. "Telepho-o-o-one!"

Madison stopped typing at the keyboard and
held her breath.

It couldn't be Mark on the phone . . . could it?

She trotted off to pick up the line, head swimming with thoughts about what she would say if
Mark were on the other end.

What if he was calling to say that he missed see-
ing Madison that afternoon and could they do something else together tomorrow?

What if he was calling at that exact moment to
talk about the Fourth of July?

Her heart skipped a beat when she imagined his
voice and his funny laugh. "Hello?" she whispered
into the receiver.

"Maddie?" the voice on the other end whispered
back. "Honey bear?"

It wasn't Mark. It was Mom!

"Mom!" Madison was glad to hear her mom's
voice. "What's going on?"

Mom explained that she was still in San Francisco,
but she'd been in so many meetings for the last day
that she could barely get away. Tonight, however,

she said, was reserved for a conversation with her favorite person on the planet.

Madison.

"How's Gramma Helen's?" Mom inquired. "She told me that you made a new friend."

"Oh, that," Madison said. "Yeah, I met this kid who lives nearby."

"Sounds like fun," Mom said. Madison could almost hear her smiling over the telephone wires.

"What's new in San Francisco?" Madison asked.

"It's hilly!" Mom said, chuckling. "But it's such a beautiful place. We'll have to come here together sometime. You'd love the streetcars and parks and the Golden Gate Bridge."

Madison thought about how Bigwheels said she'd be on that bridge this week, too. She wished she were there to see her mom and her keypal at the same time.

"I miss you, Mom," Madison admitted. "I mean, I'm having a great time with Gramma. But it's raining today and I miss you."

"I heard about that rain!" Mom said. "The bad weather should pass by the time the Fourth of July hits. You'll have your fireworks display, Maddie!"

Madison told Mom about what they had planned in Winnetka Village for the Independence Day celebration. Mom said it all sounded wonderful.

"And what else have you been up to?" Mom

asked. "Is Gramma pulling everything out of her bag of tricks?"

Madison told Mom about playing cards every day, about her morning trip to the beach, and about the surprise discovery in the shed that afternoon.

"The shed? You mean Grandpa's shed?" Mom asked.

"Yeah," Madison said. "I found something interesting on the wall in there. Something *you* carved into the wood like a million years ago."

Mom gasped. "What is it?"

"You wrote all over the wall in there, Mom," Madison said. "Fran loves Ethan. That kind of stuff."

Mom started to giggle—hard.

"What are you laughing at?" Madison asked. She wished she could see the look on Mom's face.

"Myself . . . you . . . that place," Mom said. "See? I told you Gramma's was full of surprises."

"Well, that wall sure surprised me," Madison said.

"I love you so much, honey bear," Mom said softly.

The phone clicked for a second like Mom had been disconnected, but she was still there, still laughing.

Madison realized she wasn't really drowning at all, like she'd written in her files. For one thing, she had Gramma close by.

And near or far, Mom would always be there to keep her safer than safe.

Chapter 11

Madison rubbed the sleep out of her eyes as she and Phin strolled around Gramma's backyard the next morning. Phin was restless, probably because he'd been cooped up with all the rain the day before. It was earlier than early, too, and Madison didn't think anyone else was awake. She wore her nightshirt, pj bottoms, and flip-flops (even though they were still a little bit muddy from yesterday's downpours).

Mist spread out like a blanket over the entire ground. The whole yard was like one damp prism; Madison saw little rainbows everywhere the dew collided with morning light. It was like Mom said. There was magic hidden all over the place at Gramma's cottage.

"Madison!" a voice called out to her from across the yard.

She knew the voice and turned around. Mark was standing there.

"Mark?" she called back, crossing her arms so he wouldn't see what she was wearing. She didn't even want to think about what her hair looked like. She took a deep breath and wished he would walk away.

But he came closer!

"Hey!" Mark said. "I am so sorry that I couldn't hang out yesterday. My grandmother had to wait around for her doctor . . . and then we had to go to this pharmacy . . . and then we went out to eat."

Madison nodded at everything he said without saying much herself. She had an instant urge to RUN, RUN, RUN. After all, she was wearing pajamas! But she stood right there, a stick in the mud.

"Hey!" Mark pointed to her shirt and came a little closer. "Do you like *The Simpsons*? That's my favorite show."

"Yeah, I like *The Simpsons*," she said.

He shifted around awkwardly. Was he nervous— or was he just *embarrassed* about Madison's hideous outfit?

"Maybe can we hang out today," Mark said. "My grandmother says we can play tennis at the club down the road. She has guest passes for both of us. And they have extra rackets if you need one."

"Um . . . okay . . . sure . . . but . . . I have to go inside now. . . ." Madison said, her voice drifting off a little. She tried desperately to edge away from Mark so he wouldn't get too close. They agreed to meet an hour later for tennis.

Madison wanted to evaporate. She couldn't believe that Mark had seen her like that! Since he didn't seem to care, she convinced herself that she wouldn't care, either—at least not this once—but it didn't make the encounter any less embarrassing.

Afterward Madison knew she *had* to fix her hair up nice and put on some real clothes. She found some white shorts and pulled on a blue T-shirt. It wasn't the same one she'd worn to the beach, but she liked the way it looked. After trying unsuccessfully to fix her hair in pigtails, she finally shoved it all up into the tortoiseshell clip. It was *definitely* a better outfit than her pj's.

Phinnie whined a little bit when he realized that Madison would be leaving him behind and he'd miss an afternoon outdoors. He saw her pulling on sneakers, something Madison usually only did when the two of them went on long walks together.

"Fwroooooorf," Phin snorted, and crouched down on the rug.

She patted his head and tried to put his pug mind at ease.

"I'm just going to play tennis for an hour or so," Madison said. "And when I come back, we can hang out together with Gramma Helen."

As soon as the doorbell rang, she kissed Gramma

good-bye on the forehead and dashed out the door to meet Mark. He was standing there on the stoop of Gramma's cottage in a white tennis outfit, as though he was a professional player or something, swinging his graphite racket.

"Hey, there!" Madison said, bouncing out the front door. "I'm all set to beat you!" she teased.

Mark lightly hit her shoulder, teasing back. "Don't even try it," he joked.

Madison, of course, hit him right back. "No, I'm going to BEAT you," she said, giggling.

They were both blushing. Madison could tell. Her own cheeks felt hot, and Mark's looked pink. Or was that sunburn?

It took them only twenty minutes to walk to the courts. When they arrived, no one else was playing, which was a big bonus. They could choose any court they wanted. Madison borrowed a racket from the clubhouse and grabbed a couple of tennis balls before heading out to court six.

They played in silence for most of the beginning games. Mark was trying to hit all the shots. He sent a couple of balls whizzing past Madison's head. She dunked a few lobs into his backcourt. Soon they were in the middle of a "real" set, keeping score and everything.

"What's the score again?" Madison asked, ready to toss the tennis ball into the air for a serve.

"Love–thirty," Mark said.

Madison fixated on the way he said the word *love*. She loved it.

Then she hit a serve that bounced out-of-bounds.

"Love–forty," Mark said.

Madison rolled a tennis ball between her two fingers before launching it into the air.

Thwack!

No sooner had the ball landed in the opposite court than Mark swatted at it and hit back a perfect return.

"Game to me!" he yelled when Madison missed hitting back the ball by a mile. "Now we have to switch sides."

The total score was four games to none, his advantage.

Madison was glad to feel so cheerful that morning; otherwise, she would have felt utterly defeated.

As they swapped net sides, they passed each other and Mark tapped Madison on the shoulder as if to say, "Hey!" They went on playing at the club for another hour and a half—almost twice as much time as Madison had anticipated. By the time they decided to call it quits, she was sweating from the sun right through her blue T-shirt, so Madison made extra sure that she didn't turn around in front of Mark. She'd endured enough humiliating outfits for one day.

On the walk home, Mark stopped his teasing, though, and got serious all of a sudden.

"I wanted to ask you something," Mark started to say. "I've been thinking . . ."

Madison was listening, although she was a little more focused on keeping her stride behind Mark's. She didn't want him to catch sight of her sweaty shirt—and the way he was talking was making her a little nervous.

"Well . . ." Mark said, slowing down his pace so Madison could catch up. "Since we've been hanging out together this week anyway . . ."

Madison smiled. "Yes?" she said, following him like she was doing some kind of dance.

"I've been wanting to ask you this since the day at the beach," Mark said, stopping short.

"What?" Madison asked. She stopped walking, too.

"Do you want to go to the Fourth of July fireworks?" he asked.

Madison's insides thumped. "You mean *together*?" she asked, bolder once again than she'd ever been with Hart Jones.

Mark shrugged. "Well, yeah," he said.

"I'm not sure," Madison said. "I don't really know if . . ."

"It doesn't have to be a big deal. I mean, I didn't mean to make a big d-d-deal out of it. . . ." Now Mark was stuttering. He was definitely *nervous*.

"I'd really *like* to go," Madison started to say. "But . . ."

"But?" Mark asked.

Madison could hear herself thinking and then speaking in stereo. It was as if she'd been propelled outside her own body to watch herself walking down the street. She wanted to scream, "YES, OF COURSE I WILL GO WITH YOU!"

But that wasn't what she replied.

"Well, I would love to go with you, but I really think I should spend the Fourth of July with my gramma Helen. I came here to visit her, after all. It seems funny to go to the fireworks without her. Don't you agree?"

"I guess," Mark said. "Yeah."

Madison surprised herself. She'd taken his invitation—the first offer she'd ever gotten like that *ever*—and said no?

Mark looked like he couldn't believe it, either.

By now, they'd reached their grandmothers' houses.

"Well, I guess I'll see you around," Mark said to Madison.

"Okay," Madison replied. "See you."

She watched him walk back over to his grandmother's yard without saying another word. He didn't even wave before heading inside.

Madison walked into the front hall to find Gramma leaned over Phinnie, brushing his coat. He was panting happily.

"How was tennis?" Gramma asked.

Madison told her what had happened at the courts. She said that on the way home Mark had "sort of" asked her to go to the Fourth of July celebration.

"Sort of?" Gramma asked.

"Yeah," Madison said. "I mean—it's not like a date or anything."

"Of course it isn't!" Gramma said. "So when are you two meeting?"

"Well, we're not meeting. Because I said no," Madison explained. "I told him I was already going with someone. You."

Gramma leaned over and stroked Madison's head. "Oh, Maddie!" she said. "Maddie, Maddie, Maddie!"

Madison snickered. "Cut it out, Gramma. That tickles."

"I want you to go over to Mabel's house right this second and tell that young man that you've changed your mind . . ." Gramma said in an animated voice.

"Huh? I can't do that," Madison said.

"Why not?"

"Because . . . I already said no. And it's too embarrassing," Madison said. "To go all the way over to his house . . ."

"Well, then, fine. Tell him at dinner," Gramma said.

"Dinner?" Madison asked.

"Mabel and Mark are coming here for supper. I

invited them both while you two were off playing tennis."

"Gramma!" Madison wailed. "You didn't!"

"You know, you should really trust your grand-mother when it comes to this sort of thing," Gramma replied. "Now, it's four-thirty. Dinner is in an hour."

"An hour? Here?"

Madison glanced up at the clock on the wall and groaned. She made an exasperated face at Gramma and ran up the center stairs toward her room. Phin followed closely behind, pug tail curling all the way.

She wasn't sure if she would change her mind about Mark's invitation, but Madison *did* know that she needed to take a shower. Mark had already seen her in pj's and this sweaty blue T-shirt today. The least Madison could do was to look nicer than nice for the surprise dinner.

The dinner guests arrived at five-thirty sharp.

Mabel was gabbing like crazy when she entered, but Mark didn't say much at all. And he said even less at dinner, except to ask for salt and pepper twice.

Something had really changed between him and Madison since that afternoon. Although she hadn't meant to, she'd hurt Mark's feelings by saying no to his Fourth of July request.

Madison considered Gramma's advice. Should she

130

tell him she *would* go to see the fireworks now? Wouldn't changing her mind to say yes right now in the middle of dinner leave Mark twice as confused about what was going on?

Madison didn't know *what* to say.

She was swallowed up by a bad case of nerves—more nerves than she'd ever had with a boy in her entire life—more than Hart, Drew, and Egg put together.

Was it better to let the grandmothers do all the talking?

Mabel didn't help matters much. She hadn't hushed up since she came into the house, chattering on and on. Madison figured she just loved to hear the sound of her own voice. While Mark sat there silently picking at his meat loaf and peas, Mabel shared embarrassing stories of his childhood.

Madison was horrified. At one point, she tried to catch his eye, to give him a smile so he wouldn't be embarrassed by the attention, but Mark didn't flinch.

Thankfully, Gramma didn't bring up any of *Madison's* childhood traumas in the middle of their conversations. Instead she actually tried to change the subject, getting Mabel to talk about bridge, painting, and other activities coming up at the Winnetka Village Senior Center.

Before they knew it, Gramma Helen was serving coffee and cookies. The evening was winding down—and Madison had survived.

Or at least she thought so.

On her way out the door, Mabel suddenly said in a very loud voice, "So, what are you two doing tomorrow?"

Madison's eyes opened wide. "Tomorrow?" she asked.

"For the Fourth of July!" Mabel said, grinning. "There's a lot going on in town."

"Nothing," Mark said quickly. "Except going to the fireworks with you, Grams."

"That's all?" Mabel said.

"I think you two should go to the fireworks together," Gramma Helen interrupted. "It's so much more fun for the younger crowd. Mabel and I will just be boring companions. Don't you think, Mabel?" She elbowed her friend.

"You're not boring," Madison said, giving her gramma a look.

"Ooooh no! I agree with Helen," Mabel said. "We're a pair of old fogies."

"You're not fogies," Mark chimed in.

"Now, I said I agree with Helen, and that's all there is to it!" Mabel said assertively. "This is an event for the kids, not for us old folks. And you two are the ones who have to go together. It will be *fun*."

Madison looked at Mark.

Mark looked at Madison.

Mabel grabbed her purse. "Well, I think this decision is made. You two are going, and that's that. No argument, right? Right!"

"Grams . . ." Mark started to say, but he cut himself off, scratching his head. "Whatever."

Madison could feel her whole body get clammy, like all her nerves were operating at full tilt. "Okay." She sighed.

Gramma Helen sensed her discomfort.

"How about we *all* go together," Gramma Helen suggested. "And then you two kids can go off to the barbecue by yourselves. How does that sound?"

Madison looked at Mark.

Mark looked at Madison.

And *that* was that.

Chapter 12

The sun rose hot and glaring on the morning of the Fourth of July. The air was stickier than sticky, too, and Madison had less than no idea what to wear. She tried on every pair of shorts and pants she'd packed, testing out color combinations and matching clothes with her different sandals. When she finally decided on the right outfit, she sat down at her laptop and headed straight for bigfishbowl.com.

There was e-mail waiting from Bigwheels—just as Madison had hoped there would be.

```
From: Bigwheels
To: MadFinn
Subject: Re: I am in LIKE
Date: Thur 3 July 8:18 PM
```

That guy sounds nice and you
DEFINITELY have to send me a
picture. But what happened to
Hart from home? Do you still like
him, too? You are lucky—it sounds
like the best summer vacation
ever!

Yesterday we drove over the Golden
Gate Bridge and all this fog rolled
in while we were there. It was
cool. My little sister got sick,
though, so Mom and Dad are thinking
of heading home early. That stinks,
but this is a long trip and
everyone in the camper is totally
grouchy.

How is your grandmother? Did you
end up bringing the dog w/you? Has
Phin ever been on a plane?

The survey you sent to me is
attached. Send me one back ASAP!
HAPPY JULY 4 TO YOU!

Yours till the bubble gums,

Bigwheels

<Attachment: whatrulike.doc2>

Madison quickly opened the document with the survey questions. It wasn't a big deal; she was just curious.

<u>WHAT R U LIKE?</u>

Name	Victoria
Nickname	Vicki
Screen name	Bigwheels
Home	Washington State
Favorite color	Blue
Favorite ice cream	Lemon sherbet
Hobbies	Computers, reading
Lucky number	8
Pets	Nope
Brothers and sisters	1 sister + 1 brother
Favorite subject	English
I want to travel to...	Visit Madison!
Best friend	My keypal Madison!

Everything Bigwheels sent was stuff Madison already knew, except for the "I want to travel to" and "best friend" parts. They were a huge surprise.

Madison clicked REPLY and sent her own survey back along with a note.

From: MadFinn
To: Bigwheels
Subject: Thanks a bunch
Date: Fri 4 July 10:30 AM

Happy Independence Day 2 U! Thanks for the survey. I got it and here's mine—I cut & pasted it below. I

hope you get 2 see a parade or
something tonite.

Yours till the fire crackers,

MadFinn

<u>WHAT R U LIKE?</u>

Name	Madison
Nickname	Maddie
Screen name	MadFinn
Home	Far Hills, New York
Favorite color	NEON ORANGE!!!
Favorite ice cream	Cherry Garcia
Hobbies	Animals, computers, writing in my files
Lucky number	11
Pets	Phinnie, my pug
Brothers and sisters	None
Favorite subject	Science and computers
I want to travel to ...	The moon LOL
Best friend	Aimee, Fiona, and my keypal Bigwheels

After hitting SEND, Madison glanced up at the
digital clock. It said 10:47.

No more e-mails and notes to Bigwheels!

No more changing outfits!

The morning was slowly vanishing, and the
moment of truth had come. She needed to get ready
for her Fourth of July date—for real.

Even Phin barked his approval when Madison got dressed in the lacy blue shirt she had borrowed from Fiona. It fit perfectly, and she wore it with faded jeans instead of shorts, just in case the bugs started biting while they were sitting on the lawn at night. To top everything off, Madison put on the moonstone earrings that Dad had given her for good luck. She was sure she needed luck to get through the evening with Mark.

Gramma was in the kitchen, putting together a basket of food and other goodies for the afternoon and evening. They'd agreed to meet up on the main lawn near Tower Head Beach Park. Mabel and Gramma Helen would sit around chatting and playing cards into the evening, while Madison and Mark went over to the carnival and rode rides.

Around four-thirty, the doorbell to Gramma's house rang.

Mark was standing outside, holding a blanket.

"You guys ready to go?" he asked Madison through the screen door.

"Yeah, we are," Madison said, fidgeting.

She wanted to say more. She needed to tell Mark that she was sorry for what had happened the day before, but she held it inside. She hoped they would have a chance to talk more once they got to the celebration.

"Let me get Gramma," was all Madison said. "Wait here."

Downtown Winnetka Village was decorated to the hilt with streamers and balloons and bright bunches of flowers. A brass quartet had set itself up in the band shell. Men and women were arranging chairs into straight rows all the way back as far as the eye could see. Volunteers dressed up as Uncle Sam handed out miniature flags to everyone who passed by.

Madison, Mark, Gramma, Mabel, and Phinnie walked slowly along the edge of the sidewalk, careful not to bump into any of the spectators who were lining the street. Since the morning parade, the people had stayed three deep up and down the park. This event was the most popular event in town all year, Mabel said. People arrived from surrounding counties and from Chicago to see the bands, the costumes, and, of course, the fireworks.

Phin was overwhelmed by the spectacle. He dragged his little pug body along, shaking a little because the crowd made him nervous. But the sounds and smells had his nose sniffing the air like mad.

Music played from speakers set up near city hall.

Cotton candy, barbecue, and fried dough vendors shouted for customers.

Other dogs (besides Phin) scooted in and out of the crowd.

The sensory overload left Madison a little overwhelmed, too. She hardly had any time at all to talk with Mark or even Gramma Helen. She spent more time checking to see that no one was stepping on her pug.

"Look over there!" Gramma Helen said, pointing to a painted sign that read CARNIVAL TICKETS HERE.

Before anyone could say another word, Mark was weaving his way over toward the sign. The rest of the group followed.

The carnival wasn't as big as the one in Far Hills, but it still had all the best rides. There were teacups for younger kids, a Ferris wheel, and a whirly ride that looked too scary and rickety to attempt. Both grandmothers voiced their concerns about the ride safety, of course.

In addition to rides, there was the Fourth of July Fun House, the Spooky Mansion, and the Red-White-and-Blue Maze, which people wandered through to get to the flag at the center. Madison was excited to try the last one.

"We'll find a nice shady spot under some trees," Gramma said, smiling. "And you two can find us in time for supper and the fireworks. Okay?"

Madison pointed to a giant elm tree across the park. It wasn't so crowded over there. Mabel approved.

"Now, don't get into any trouble," Mabel said, getting the last word. "We'll be right there if you need us."

Mark just smiled and shuffled forward in the ticket line.

Madison handed off Phin's leash to Gramma Helen and said her good-byes to both of them.

A few moments later, Madison and Mark were at the front of the line, still not talking. But Mark finally broke the silence.

"You don't have to stay around here," Mark said. "If you want to be with your grandmother."

Madison shook her head. "Well, no, I don't. But I want to."

"Huh?" Mark asked. He was next in line for the ticket counter.

"I want to be here. I—I mean, if you're okay with that," Madison said, stammering just like he'd been doing the day before.

"Well, I'm okay," Mark said.

"TICKETS, PLEASE! NEXT!" the silver-haired man behind the counter yelled out.

Mark and Madison scrambled up to the window and got tickets for everything except the whirly ride. Mark wanted to try it, but Madison convinced him not to do it.

"Then where do we go first?" Mark asked.

Madison felt shy all of a sudden, as if she had had the wind knocked out of her. "I don't know. . . ." she said.

"Do you want to try that maze?" he asked. "It seems cool."

"Okay, that sounds good," Madison said, not really making a decision.

"Fine, let's go," Mark said. He ran ahead. They would have to wait in another line there.

"I can't believe how crowded it is," Madison said once she caught up to him.

"Yeah, it's like this every year," Mark explained. "Usually I just go around on all the rides by myself. I plow through the people. It's easy when you're alone."

"Oh," Madison said, wondering if he liked it better alone than with her.

Mark could read her mind. He shook his head. "No, I didn't mean it like that. What I meant was—"

"Mark, I'm really sorry about the other day," Madison blurted.

"Huh?" he said.

"I'm sorry that I acted so weird. I just didn't know what to say. I get like that sometimes."

"That's cool," Mark replied. "I mean, you're not totally weird."

Madison laughed. "Not *totally*?"

"Well, you're not as weird as my grams, right?" Mark joked. "I think you're really nice."

Madison's chest expanded with the compliment. She got her wind back.

"You're nice, too," she said sweetly.

All at once, Mark started to jump around like he was excited or nervous or both. He switched subjects instantly.

"Race you through the maze!" Mark said, pulling out the wad of tickets from his pocket.

Madison threw her hands into the air. "Sure," she said. "Whoever gets there first . . ."

But before she could finish her thought, the race was on. Once they stepped inside the entry gate, Mark zoomed around a corner to get to the middle of the maze. Madison took another route, bumping into other kids and parents along the way. Although the sun was in her eyes, she managed to find the middle first. There was a giant flagpole there. She leaned up against it.

Mark straggled in a few moments later, grinning. He knew he'd been beat.

"Around that first turn . . . man . . ." he said, breathless. "I kept running into dead ends!"

"Where do you want to go next?" Madison asked.

"Let's ride the Ferris wheel," he suggested.

Once again, they were really talking—back to being summer vacation friends.

After the Ferris wheel (which got a little stuck while they were rocking in the seat at the top of the wheel), a spin around the teacups (which made Madison dizzier than dizzy), and a walk through the Fun House (which Mark rated "lamest" on a scale of "lame to lamest"), they made their way back through the crowds toward the old elm tree.

People had blankets and chairs pitched every-where. Dogs raced around, and picnic baskets still lit-tered the lawn even though it was getting late.

Madison could see Gramma Helen and Mabel from far across the park.

"This is really fun," Mark told Madison on their way back. "I'm glad you're here."

Madison blushed. "Thanks. Me too."

"But I shouldn't have eaten that last batch of fried dough," Mark said, rubbing his belly. He burped, and Madison laughed. For some reason, it didn't gross her out the same way it did when Egg or Hart burped.

"Well, look at YOU!" Mabel said, putting down her hand of cards to wave hello to Mark and Madison as they approached.

"How was the carnival?" Gramma Helen asked with a big smile.

Madison smiled back. "Fun," she said. "We rode almost everything."

"Except the whirly ride," Mark added, grinning at Madison.

She nodded and blushed, then bent down to pet Phin, who was rolling around on the cool grass.

The sky slowly turned from pink to gray as dusk approached. Everyone around the elm tree was settling onto their blankets in preparation for the evening's musical performance and fireworks. Madison found an open spot to sit on the corner of Mabel's enormous quilt. Mark sat on the opposite corner.

As darkness fell, the trumpets started to play. Gramma Helen hummed along to George Gershwin's *Rhapsody in Blue*. Mabel tried to hum, too, but her humming was loud and a little off-key. Madison was sure that everyone was staring.

Around nine o'clock, the first official Fourth of July rocket shot into the air and exploded in an arc of white and blue. Gramma Helen reached for Phin, who barked and shoved his nose under the blanket. He was scared of the *booms*.

Madison, on the other hand, squeaked with delight.

"This is pretty cool, huh?" Mark whispered, edging a little closer to Madison's corner of the quilt without seeming to realize it.

Madison nodded in the half dark. "Uh-huh," she said. "It's like magic."

Ka-boom!

More fireworks exploded in the skies over the park and over Lake Michigan.

Ka-boom!

The crowd gasped and sighed in unison.

At one point, Phinnie tried to dart away. Madison threw herself across the quilt to catch onto his collar. Her knees touched Mark's as she fell forward.

"Phin!" she yelled, picking herself up. She was practically in Mark's lap, but he wasn't moving away.

"Whoops," he said in a doofy voice.

Madison giggled nervously. "Yeah, whoops." She pushed herself upright and grabbed ahold of Phin's collar and leash for good.

Ka-boom! Boom! Boom!

"Are you two having fun?" Mabel yelled out. "Isn't this spectacular?"

Mark looked at Madison, and he didn't look away, not even to see what was exploding next. She could see the flash of fireworks across his nose and chin—a blur of whites and greens and purples all at the same time. Her stomach flip-flopped like it had never flip-flopped before.

Ka-boom!

This was the Fourth of July Madison had always wanted.

Chapter 13

 Fireworks

I don't know how to write this down. My hands are shaking. All of me is shaking.

I guess I will just say it:

Mark kissed me.

HE KISSED ME AND I KISSED HIM BACK!

I haven't told a soul. I don't even know how I feel. It is so weird to want something for so long and then have it happen. Only it wasn't with the person I expected.

Rude Awakening: Sometimes it's better to follow my heart—not my Hart.

I have to send an e-mail to Bigwheels. She will flip out, I know. And I don't know

what Aimee and Fiona will say. They have
both had their first kisses already, so
it's no biggie for them. But it is SUCH a
huge deal for me. Mark is my new and
improved crush.

I can't believe I didn't want to come
visit Gramma.

What was I thinking?

Madison closed her file and opened her e-mail so
she could write to Bigwheels with all the details of
the first kiss.

Her hands were still shaky on the keyboard and
mouse as she wrote.

She kept spacing out in the middle of sentences,
too. All she could think about was the way Mark
looked and sounded from the night before.

She wanted to relive every moment all over
again.

From: MadFinn
To: Bigwheels
Subject: GUESS WHAT HAPPENED TO ME?
Date: Sat 5 July 9:52 AM
I hope ur trip is still happening &
that u didn't have to go home
early. Thanks for ur e-card of the
bridge, too. I think I may save it
as a screen saver when I get back 2
Far Hills. Ur the BEST!

148

N e way, the most incredible thing happened to me yesterday and I don't even know what 2 say about it so I will just tell you as many details as I can remember.

I went to the local fireworks and carnival with my gramma Helen and the boy next door and his grandmother. At first Mark and I were acting all weird together, but then we got along better and went on all these rides. He is so funny and cute. I had all these butterflies in my tummy while we were hanging out together.

Sometimes I think you just KNOW when something cool is about to happen, you know? I felt that way yesterday.

I was so right.

He KISSED me. Can you believe it? Right there in my gramma Helen's backyard, too. We came back from the fireworks and we were walking Phinnie around before we said good-bye. Earlier that night we had

been sitting close and I felt all
tingly. You know that feeling? N e
way, as we were walking around the
yard, our hands sort of touched
and then we were actually HOLDING
hands. His was a little sweaty,
but that is okay because it's
July, right? And maybe mine was
sweaty, too.

We held hands for almost ten
minutes. I could feel my heart
beating faster. And just before he
went back over to his grandmother's
house, he squeezed my hand and
leaned in and kissed me. Okay, he
actually kissed half my mouth and
part of my cheek, but it was so
nice. I think I froze up a little
bit because he moved back with
this strange look on his face
like, "What did I do wrong?"

That's when I leaned forward a
little bit and we kissed again.
This time it was really on the
lips. It only lasted a split
second, but he had really soft
lips, I could tell that much. I
CAN'T BELIEVE THIS HAPPENED TO ME!

And I can't believe I have to see
him again today. I want to sooo
much, but I don't know what to say.

What do you say to someone who
kissed you?

What if one and a half kisses
didn't matter to him as much as me?

I will keep you updated after I
figure out what to do. Write back
sooner than soon, ok?

Yours till the lip sticks,

MadFinn

p.s. :X (or else)

Madison hit SEND and put her laptop into its
snooze function. She wanted to write more, but she
had to eat some breakfast first. Gramma was sipping
a cup of tea. Phin was asleep at her feet in the din-
ing room.

"Good morning!" Gramma said in her cheeriest
voice as Madison shuffled into the kitchen in her pj's.
"I made some pancakes."

Madison smiled. Pancakes were another food
that was hard to eat without feeling happy. Mom

always made them to celebrate a special occasion. Gramma could probably tell this was one of those.

"So the Fourth of July celebration was fun last night, wasn't it?" Gramma asked.

Madison nodded and took a bite of blueberry pancakes smothered in syrup. "Mmmnuh-huh," she mumbled with a mouthful of food.

"That Mark is *such* a sweet boy," Gramma said, winking.

Phinnie jumped up on Madison's knee, begging for his own bite of pancake. Madison sneaked him a bite under the table.

"He's nice," Madison answered, barely able to contain her grin.

"You know what? I think he likes you, Maddie," Gramma whispered, like she was giving away a big secret. "You can tell by the way he looks at you."

"Gramma!" Madison exclaimed, embarrassed. "He does not."

Gramma shook her head. *"Tsk, tsk, tsk,"* she clucked. "I think he does."

Mark's face popped into Madison's thoughts again. She could feel the way last night felt all over again: the warm temperature, the smell of barbecue, the sounds of fireworks exploding, and the way it felt to hold hands. . . .

"Oh—don't forget that your mom wants you to call her later," Gramma reminded Madison. "You'll have to tell her the big news."

"What big news?" Madison said, playing dumb. "I don't know what you're talking about, Gramma."

Gramma Helen grinned again. "Oh, well, you know me. I don't know what I'm talking about. I guess I'll just clear away these dishes, then." She wandered into the kitchen with a stack of plates.

"Why were you saying that?" Madison asked, chasing after her. Phin followed closely behind.

Standing by the sink, Gramma started humming *Rhapsody in Blue* the way she had the night before. "I don't know. Maybe you should go visit Mark and see what he's up to today?" she hinted.

Madison wrinkled her eyebrows together. "Gramma!" she said, unable to hold back her smile. "I can't believe that you think—"

She cut herself off.

Of course Gramma knew that there were more sparks going off in Winnetka that night than the ones in the air over the park.

"Looks like another sunny day today, doesn't it?" Gramma said.

Madison gave her a big bear hug. "You're the best, Gramma," she cooed, squeezing hard.

"So are you, dearie," Gramma replied, kissing Madison's head. "So are you."

Mabel answered the bell when Madison rang it over at the house next door.

"My, my!" Mabel said, opening the door wide.

"Come on in! I didn't think I'd see *you* so bright and early today!"

Madison walked in slowly, glancing around for signs of Mark.

"Yeah, I got up early today," Madison said. "Um . . . is Mark around?"

"Yes indeed," Mabel said. "He's just packing up all of his stuff."

"Packing?" Madison asked.

Mabel frowned. "Oh, didn't he tell you? He's going back to his parents in Chicago today. My ankle seems to be doing better, so he's headed home. I sure will miss him. . . ."

At that exact moment, Mark came into the room. His eyes lit up when he saw Madison standing there. "Hey!" he cried with a smile.

But Madison wasn't sure what to say now that she'd learned he was leaving Winnetka. "Hey," she mumbled.

"What's up?" he asked.

"Oh, nothing. I was just coming over to see if maybe you wanted to hang out . . . but your grandmother tells me you're leaving . . . and gee, I guess. . . ."

She tripped over her words.

Mark shook his head. "No! I'm just packing up because my dad told me to be ready later today. I'm not *actually* leaving here until after six. That's when he's coming to get me."

154

The phone rang and Mabel hurried to answer it, leaving the two of them alone together. The room was quieter than quiet.

"So . . ." Madison said.

"So . . ." Mark said.

"Want to go for a walk with me and Phinnie?" she asked. "I know it's in the middle of everything, but . . ."

"Yeah, sure," Mark said. "We can walk the beach up to the dog. I mean, we can walk the dog up to the beach."

Madison giggled.

He grabbed his baseball cap and they went back next door to Gramma Helen's to get Phin. He was extra playful that morning, so they had their hands full walking him down the busy road and over to the beach.

Everywhere Madison looked, she saw signs of the preceding day's events: burnt-out sparklers, deadwood bonfire branches, and rusty cans. There had been a huge Fourth of July party on the beach as well as the park. The cleanup crew would probably be arriving soon.

The pair kicked sand and rocks out of the way as they paraded down the beach with Phin. Mark picked up a giant pinecone and handed it to Madison.

After strolling along for twenty minutes or so, they finally stopped to sit by the dunes. Phin roamed in and out of the grass that grew wild up and down the beach nearby. Madison had his doggy leash hooked onto a bench to keep an eye on him.

"This is a nice beach," Mark said. "I came here when I was little."

Madison pushed a loose strand of hair behind her ear. "What was it like then?" she asked.

"Pretty much the same," Mark said. "It seemed bigger, though." He smiled.

"I hate to leave," Madison admitted. "To go back to Far Hills and Lake Dora. That lake isn't as much fun as this one. That's for sure."

"I wish I didn't have to leave, either," Mark said. "This trip has been better than I expected."

"I wish you didn't have to leave, either," Madison joined in.

"Yeah, it was cool that we met," Mark said.

All at once, he reached out and took Madison's hand all over again, only his hand wasn't so sweaty this time. She grabbed on to it tightly and then glanced around to see if anyone was spying. Of course, no one was even looking.

"Maybe we'll both be here just visiting at the same time some other time?" she asked.

Mark nodded. "Maybe. Do you have e-mail?"

Madison laughed out loud. "Of course I have e-mail!" she said. "I love computers."

"Yeah, I'm in the computer club at school," Mark said.

"You *are*?" Madison asked. She couldn't believe that through all their conversations over the past few days, neither of them had mentioned her favorite thing in the world.

"So I'll write if you give me your e-mail address," he promised. "If you'll write back."

Madison giggled. "Of course I will."

Phin started barking at something in the sand, and they turned around to see him attacking (or trying to attack) a stick. The stick was winning.

"Rrrrrrrrrrrooooooooooff!" the dog wailed, jumping around so much that he sent sand flying in every direction. Madison ran over to calm him down.

"I think I better get back home," Mark said. "Grams needed help with some other things before I go."

"Your dad is coming to pick you up?" Madison asked.

"Yeah, we live pretty close, actually, in the city. I told you that, right?"

Madison nodded. "You did."

"Anyway . . ." Mark said, standing up. "I'm heading back."

But he didn't move.

Madison stood up, too.

"I really should hang out here with Phinnie for a while," Madison said. "He's so hyper today for some reason. And we're leaving tomorrow, so—"

"Well, good-bye, then," Mark said abruptly.

"Good-bye, then," Madison said.

Mark reached out to give Madison a hug but missed and ended up craning his neck out over her shoulder, so it felt like more of a lean than a hug. He didn't hold on for very long, either—and laughed a little as he pulled away.

Nothing was really *funny*. It was just jitters. Now Madison was the one making the boy nervous.

Madison pulled her handmade card out of her pocket and handed it to Mark. He smiled and took it.

Phinnie howled as Mark turned and trudged up the beach, waving one last good-bye. Madison tried to tell the dog to be quiet, but then Phin started to jump around and she got distracted. By the time Madison looked up to see Mark walking away again, he was gone completely from her view.

The water was calm except for a light breeze that rippled across the surface. Madison noticed all the colors in Lake Michigan at once—not just blues anymore, but greens and yellows and cloudy whites.

The magic really was here.

And she finally had some to call her very own.

Chapter 14

"Did you pack all the clothes we did in the wash yesterday?" Gramma Helen asked Madison as she closed her suitcase. "I left a folded pile downstairs for you."

"I think I have everything," Madison said, sitting on the edge of the bed before she zipped her luggage.

At her feet, Phin was stretched out on the floor, panting. He knew something strange was going on. He had a sixth sense about suitcases. Madison wondered if he knew another airplane ride was in his future.

"Is this yours?" Gramma asked. She was holding the pinecone from the beach.

Madison took it and smiled. "Oh yes." She carefully wrapped it in a tissue from the nightstand and placed it into her airplane carry-on bag. She hoped her laptop wouldn't squash it.

Gramma's eyes got a little wet again. "I wish you could visit me more often," she sniffled. "I hate to see you go."

"Oh, Gramma!" Madison said, burying her head in Gramma's side, which smelled just like the roses from her car.

"I'm just a sentimental old mush, aren't I?" Gramma said, still sniffling. "But you're getting so big, and soon you'll be all grown up. Where has the time gone?"

"Playing crazy eights," Madison joked. "That's where!"

Gramma laughed out loud. "Everyone here loved meeting you," she said. "Especially Mabel. And she said that Mark *liked* you very much. He didn't want to go back to Chicago yesterday. How about that?"

Madison smiled. "Really?" she said.

"Really," Gramma said, winking. "Told you so."

Gramma helped Madison carry the bags to the front door. She handed her a pouch for the plane ride with two peanut-butter sandwiches and some green grapes. There were two sandwiches because Madison would be meeting Mom on the flight home. She'd be connecting upon her return from San Francisco. Madison was glad she wouldn't have to travel alone.

"Good-bye, Winnetka!" Madison said as they

pulled out of Gramma's driveway. She waved to Mabel's house, too.

All the way to the airport, Phin whined from his carrier. By the time Madison and Gramma left him off with the baggage handler, however, he'd tired himself out. Madison watched as he was led into the back room to board the flight.

The trip home had begun, and Madison could feel the excitement building inside her. She would miss Gramma, for sure, but she was eager to see Aimee and Fiona, her bedroom, and, of course, Mom.

They waited by their gate for Mom to appear, sipping cola and talking more about Mark, Mabel, and the fireworks from the other night. Gramma bought Madison two fashion magazines to read on the plane home, too.

"Well, here you are!" someone called out to them.

Madison looked up to see her mom walking quickly toward their gate. In her arms was a large, rectangular wrapped package that intrigued Madison. Was this a present for her? Mom put it down on the floor gently.

She embraced Gramma Helen first—and held on for a big squeeze.

"Was my daughter good?" Mom asked Gramma teasingly. She reached over and wrapped an arm around Madison's shoulders.

"She was a little troublemaker!" Gramma said, faking exasperation.

Mom raised her eyebrows and looked at Madison, who shrugged.

"That's me," Madison said. "I'm serious trouble, Mom."

The three of them laughed as an announcer pre-boarded their flight. Gramma dug around in her purse for Madison's ticket.

"Oh—this is for you, Mother," Mom said to Gramma, handing her the big package. For a split second, Madison was bummed, since she was sure the gift was for her. But she got over it. Gramma looked so surprised.

"For me?" she said, starting to sniffle all over again like she'd done at the cottage. She hugged Mom tightly. "I'm sorry we didn't spend more time together this visit, dear," she said.

Mom nodded. "Me too. But we will. You'll be coming to Far Hills soon."

"Open the present," Madison said, hopping up and down a little bit. "Gramma! Open it!"

Gramma leaned down and tore a corner off the box. It was a framed picture. Mom helped her to open it up wide.

Madison gasped. Inside was a beautiful painted portrait of Gramma Helen and Grandpa Joe. It was modeled after a photo of them from when they were much younger.

"Oh, Francine!" Gramma said, clutching her chest. Now she started to cry.

"A friend of mine is an artist in San Francisco. He's been working on this for a few months now. I picked it up from his studio while I was out there. Dad looks good in it, don't you think?" Mom asked. "And so do you."

Madison watched the two of them go back and forth over details from the painting. She didn't remember a time when they seemed so close.

Or when Madison felt closer to both of them.

"Flight two-thirteen now boarding rows fifteen and higher," the ticket attendant announced over the loudspeaker.

"That's us!" Mom said, giving her own mother another hug. "Ma, can you manage carrying this back to your car? It isn't really that heavy."

Gramma nodded, wiping her nose with a handkerchief she'd pulled out of her purse. "I'm fine. You two better shake a leg, though. Good-bye. I'll miss you both."

They gathered their carry-on bags and boarding passes and said their final good-byes. And with the walk into the plane, the surprise Fourth of July vacation officially ended.

Madison would miss this place, but she was ready to sleep in her own room again—especially if the air-conditioning was back working again.

She was ready to be with Mom and Phin alone again.

She was ready to hang out with Aimee and Fiona and the rest of her friends from FHJH again.

And that included Hart Jones—even if he *had* gone to the Fourth of July extravaganza with Poison Ivy Daly.

Settling into their seats was easy, and the plane liftoff went smoothly. After the seat-belt sign was turned off, Madison pulled out the lunch Gramma had made. She and Mom ate peanut-butter sandwiches with the free root beers the plane provided. Madison was supersurprised the airline even had root beer, but she happily drank up.

They talked about San Francisco, and then Mom worked on some data sheets and read through a script while Madison napped.

Madison was exhausted after the Fourth of July weekend—more tired than she even realized. After a short sleep, she reached into her orange bag for her book to do some reading.

That's when her pinecone fell out. Mom picked it up off the floor.

"What's this?" Mom asked, unwrapping the tissue.

Madison explained all about Tower Head Beach and crazy eights and Gramma's best friend, Mabel, in Winnetka—*and* her grandson, Mark.

"We really like each other," Madison admitted. "Mark's really cute."

Mom leaned in closer than close. "So what do

you mean by, 'we really like each other'?" she asked. "Are you and Mark going to keep in touch?"

Madison blushed. "No," she said. Then she looked deep into Mom's eyes. "Yes," she admitted. "I hope so. I don't know."

"Is there something you're not telling me?" Mom asked, grinning.

Madison wanted to share *everything* with Mom right then and there. She wanted to blab about the romantic fireworks and the kiss in Gramma's backyard and the holding hands—all of it.

But she didn't say a word more. She didn't have to.

Mom probably knew. She'd been on that same beach. She'd probably kissed Ethan Randall in that same spot in the backyard.

At that moment, Madison understood Mom better than she ever had before. And Mom understood her right back.

"So, how are your files coming along?" Mom asked next, switching subjects. "That laptop comes in handy when you have a lot to say, doesn't it?"

Madison nodded. "Dad says he's going to get me one of those cards so you can go online without a phone line. I'm not really sure how it works. . . ."

"That'll be great. Then you can e-mail friends from anywhere. Pretty soon, you'll be traveling all over just like me."

Madison always thought that was what she

wanted more than anything—to fly all over the USA and the world like Mom did for her job at Budge Films. But now, heading back to Far Hills, she was also sure that staying close to home was an even nicer thought.

She opened her laptop and went into her e-mailbox, even though it wasn't connected to the Internet right now. She needed to write to Bigwheels. She'd send it as soon as she got home.

```
From: MadFinn
To: Bigwheels
Subject: I'M ON A PLANE!!!
Date: Sun 6 July 3:09 PM
```
I am writing to you from a plane right now (isn't that cool?), row eighteen on the way back to Far Hills. Have you guys turned around to head back to Washington yet? I bet u have a long way to go in that camper. What else have you seen in California or anywhere? I've been saving all ur e-cards BTW.

Did you get my last e-mail? I am sadder than sad that I had to leave behind all the stuff that happened with that new boy I like, Mark. I wish he went to my school. Maybe

then I could know what it's like
to really have a boyfriend. Will
I ever know? Will anyone in my
"real" life ever like me like
that?

I heard that Hart went to the
Fourth of July extravaganza with
evil Poison Ivy. I'm just glad it's
summer so I don't have to watch
them hold hands like every day at
school or something weird like that.
That would be so AWFUL! What would
you do? Should I still be friends
with him even if he's dating the
enemy? Write back.

Yours till the air ports,

MadFinn

Madison hit SAVE and the message was saved
automatically into her Drafts folder. She was about
to write more e-mail, a thank-you note to Gramma
Helen, and a short hello note to Mark when the
cabin lights blinked.
The flight attendant said, "Please turn off all
electronic devices, including all personal stereos, cell
phones, and laptop computers. We will be landing
shortly."

Mom helped Madison put away the computer.

Moments later, the plane was landing and pulling into the gate, and Madison and her mom moved quickly to the baggage claim section.

"Phinnie!" they both squealed when his carrier was brought out of another side door. Madison put on his leash and he leaped around, claws and paws skidding on the airport floor.

It only took them an hour to get home once they got their suitcases and the car, which Mom had left in long-term parking.

The house looked exactly the same as it had looked when they left Far Hills. Even Phinnie was excited about heading home. Madison sat in the backseat with him so he didn't have to ride in the crate anymore.

"Rowrrooooo!" he wailed, burying his pug nose into Madison's leg with a snort.

Mom ordered pizza for dinner because there was nothing in the refrigerator. Madison laughed. Things were way back to normal here—back to Mom and her scary takeout dinners.

While Mom unpacked, Madison opened her saved message to Bigwheels. While she was waiting for it to be sent, a new e-mail addressed to Madison popped up on the screen. She knew who it was from right away because he made so many spelling mistakes.

From: TheEggMan
To: MadFinn
Subject: When r u coming home?
Date: Sun 6 July 10:10 AM

Whassup Maddie? I havnt talked to u since the lake last wk. I forgot u were going away until Fiona told me.

How was ur Grammas? I remembr her from when we were little. She was always pretty nice 2 me. N e way, everyone was bummd out that u were gone this wkend for July 4. I hung out w/the usual guys + Fiona and Aim. Chet and Hart came too, except that Hart almost went w/IVY. What a wacko. I told him to bag her and hang w/us though and he did. I used to think she was a hottie but this weekend, she was so clingy she's gross. Nothing else happend much.

Mariah my sister sez hi 2 u. call me when u come back. We want to go 2 the lake and u should be there.
L8R, Egg

Madison closed Egg's e-mail after reading it through twice more, just to be certain she was sure about what he'd said.

Hart and Ivy *hadn't* gone to the Fourth of July extravaganza together.

It was so hard to believe.

She also stayed online for a while longer just to see if maybe, by some random luck, Mark would be sending e-mail, too. He'd promised he'd write, but Madison didn't know when that would happen. She wanted him to be the first one to get in touch, though. She knew that for sure. She'd wait for *him* to make the first electronic move.

Suddenly Madison's head buzzed with boys. She liked two of them at the same time, just as Bigwheels had said. Two of them! Were Hart and Mark the real summer surprises Mom had been talking about?

Madison needed to call Aimee and Fiona and tell them about her trip home from Chicago. She needed to find out more about what had *really* happened at the Far Hills Fourth of July extravaganza.

But first, Madison went into her Summer Vacation file.

Summer Vacation

Rude awakening: This Fourth of July was MY independence day, too.

I realize now that Gramma and Mom and I are a lot alike. But I am also different.

Mom has been telling me that forever, but I finally believe her.

And maybe there are boys in the world who like me because I'm different.

I know there's one in Chicago who does.

I hope there's one at home who does, too.

Mad Chat Words:

K-I-T	Keep in touch
EOTW	End of the world
WDYS	What did you say?
{ :-{	Unhappier than unhappy
HB	Hurry back
BCNU	Be seeing you!
8 -]	Wow, man!
GR8	Great
What's gnu?	What's new?
YYSW	Yeah, yeah, sure, whatever
:X	Sworn to secrecy

Madison's Computer Tip

I thought leaving Far Hills for the Fourth of July would be the biggest drag EVER. But I was soooo wrong. **E-mail keeps me close to my BFFs, Mom and Dad, and even NEW friends when I go away.** Bigwheels sent me e-cards from all over the place on her family vacation. Aimee and Fiona sent news from home. Mom kept in touch from her business trip. And now that I met this new boy at Gramma's house, I think maybe e-mail is what will keep us connected, too.

Visit Madison at www.madisonfinn.com